African Politics & African Politicians' Behaviour on Education

(The Sierra Leone Chapter)

1961-2025

By

Mohamed Sannoh

Doctoral Researcher, UK.

Copyright

Published by

THIS PAGE IS INTENTIONALLY RESERVED AND DEDICATED TO:

HIS EXCELLENCY, THE RETIRED BRIGADIER JULIUS MAADA BIO, PRESIDENT OF THE REPUBLIC OF SIERRA LEONE, FOR MAKING MY PERSONAL DREAM COME TRUE:

“FOR PROVIDING FREE QUALITY EDUCATION FOR ALL CHILDREN IN ALL GOVERNMENT SCHOOLS IN SIERRA LEONE, EVEN WHEN NOT BORN IN SIERRA LEONE”

Table of Contents

The Author's recent publications:

Mohamed Sannoh has previously authored the following books published by Trafford Publishers in Bloomington, USA and are also obtainable at the Amazon and all online booksellers on demand.

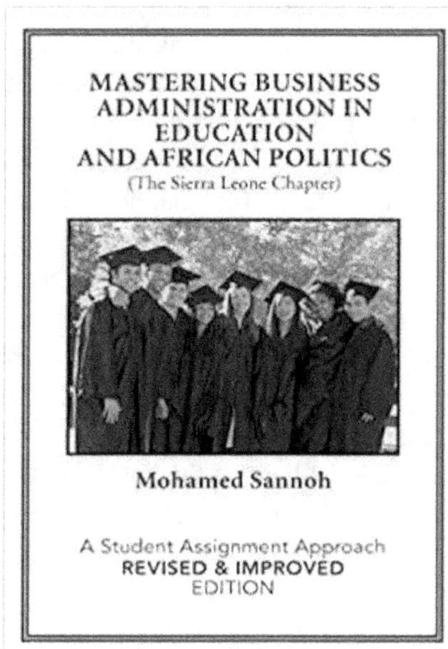

Mastering Business Administration in Education and African Politics (the Sierra Leone Chapter) This is a revised and improved edition of your book, and as I have already been told, it is quite up-to-date with far more relevant information that address education, educational business, and political issues in Africa in particular, and how these are disturbing educational developments, especially in sub-Sahara and also with suggestions for improvements.

According to Mohan Kaul, the co-chairman of Commonwealth Business Council, "given the challenges ahead, governments have realized that it is beyond their capacity and means to achieve the task of improving education for all." However, Patrick Dlamini, Chief Executive of Development Bank of South Africa, cited what has gone wrong with sudden growth of private schooling outside state control. "The government is having problems retaining seasoned teachers. Private schooling is poaching the best brains from the public schooling system, and the government is left with poor-quality teaching and inexperienced teachers because now the private sector has taken the 'crème de la crème.'

What are the origins and solutions of Africa's civil conflicts? Putting straight answers to this question, the origins of Africa's civil conflicts are

the very corrupt politicians who think that members of the civil society are at their mercy and can do nothing to stop their lootings and unfairness.

They buy houses overseas to send their children there to study, including transferring money into foreign bank accounts, leaving their people to perish, state schools and hospitals in their countries to impoverish. This happens in all African countries, including Sierra Leone, where politicians have refused to get it right. One government politician was to be appointed minister of Foreign Affairs and International Corporation in Sierra Leone, but he told the Parliamentary Committee that his credentials to substantiate his CV were to be faxed by his son from London in UK, indicating that although the politician attends Sierra Leone parliament, his family lives and supports their living expenses in UK, not in Sierra Leone.

The author of this book is bringing many experiences and especially thoughts in education from around the global, politics and religion within different and

multicultural settings but all focusing on understanding the purpose of God's world.

For those who are atheist or have never attempted to know anything about God especially when they are teachers or if they are politicians and banking on atheist ideologies of "giving the people what they want, even when not good for them" and they will vote you in, you will find this book although very irritating but educational and thought provoking.

Teachers are seriously advised to think twice before being forced into teaching ideologies that are not substantiated with written facts that are always referred to as references; otherwise they will find themselves in the job of keeping somebody in a political position, which is considered an employment seeking position. Are you ready for this?

Watch out for the next publications, printing in progress!

ATTENTION!

Many other references are consulted in the process of writing this book for your personal comforts and it is with hope that you will enjoy the facts presented here. Read it from the first cover to the last cover. Facts are deliberately presented here without biasness, and in favour of or against, any of the political parties in operation in Sierra Leone because this is the only method of exposing and educating these politicians for the benefits of our country, Sierra Leone.

We believe that the politicians who read this book will not only focus on propagating FREE QUALITY EDUCATION, but will also concentrate on providing Enough Free School Meals for our children in Sierra Leone. This is our immediate need that sustains our children in all schools.

This book is deliberately left unedited and all facts and errors explained in this book remain the responsibility of the author.

Mohamed Sannoh.

Prelude

(This book is about facts, not bias and must be read with care to understand)

Although the truth is far from being found, as Bob Woodward, the American reporter, writes in Rage (2020). This book contains different facts that other writers, such as some Sierra Leonean journalists, can hardly think of touching upon, for fear of finding themselves in hospital beds tomorrow morning and getting their enterprises boo-dozed overnight for exposing the government and the "PA".

This book is a long research presentation of different hard facts which the politicians (for over thirty years in Sierra Leone, who represent Africa in this book) think no one should dare to touch on because they have the political powers, and politicians are the ones with these political powers and they can exercise them as they wish and to their satisfaction.

Mohamed Sannoh is emerging with facts nobody or most Sierra Leoneans dare not speak about—the politics of their countries in Africa—and here, in this book, he widely and completely covered the effects of the horrors of Sierra Leone Politics and Sierra Leonean Politicians' Behaviours on education during the reign of President Siaka Stevens in Sierra Leone of the All Peoples Congress (APC) political party operations in the 1970s, when the author was a secondary school boy at the Methodist Boys' High School at Kissy Mess Mess in Freetown.

Although he agrees that the politicians have political powers, he also understands that writers, such as himself, have their professional and pen powers as well, as his former work colleague at the Methodist Boys' High School in the early 1980s, Mr Paul Kamara, will agree, when he recalls the merciless lessons that he learned that posted him on a hospital bed in London. Mohamed Sannoh is not a professional politician but a professional teacher (trained and qualified in the United Kingdom), and this title has also accorded him with the responsibility and obligation to write—not just anything, but the facts. His students learn from the facts that he teaches and enable them to pass external examinations with flying colours.

This same Mohamed Sannoh was the founder of the Institute of Commercial Management (ICM) business studies education in Sierra Leone, which was established at the Methodist Boys' High School, Kissy Mess Mess, Freetown during the days of Mr Willie Obabidon Pratt and the West African Methodist (WAM) Collegiate Secondary School at Wilkinson Road in Freetown, when the Rev. Zichriah Smith was the principal there.

Through this ICM project, he was able to assist a number of five hundred Sierra Leonean students, through the ICM Grant Award System, which gave them passages to study at the ICM College of the Business Studies Centre in Bournemouth, UK.

This same Mohamed Sannoh also registered his mark in The Gambia when he completed another ICM assignment there between 1997-2003 as the ICM Regional Co-ordinator and National Education Consultant to the Department of

Education when Hon. Ann Therese Don-Jatta was the Secretary of State for Education during the Presidency of Dr Yahya A.J.J. Jammeh. Mohamed Sannoh's responsibilities were to oversee and regularise the flow of ICM Education at educational institutions of Schools and Colleges for deliveries of ICM education programmes at the Management Development Institute (MDI), The Nusrat Senior Secondary School, and during which he further got in contact with The Gambia Technical Training Institute (GTTI), Ndow Comprehensive Secondary School, and The Glory Baptist Secondary School in New Jeswang of the Serrekunda Region. The IPAM graduation at Kairaba will never be forgotten by the many who witnessed it.

Finally, Mohamed Sannoh founded the Institute of Professional Administration and Management (IPAM-Gambia), and he was the Principal and Director of Education in 2000-2003. Mohamed Sannoh further assisted a good number of students that got admitted to pursue professional courses at other external learning institutions outside The Gambia, though he acquired educational management skills.

These are some of the reasons, in addition to others, why this book is full of facts, and if anyone finds any of the points embarrassing and difficult to cope with, there is nothing Mohamed Sannoh can do about it because he was just discharging his learned duty as a classroom teacher: to educate his students and the public about education in his country and other environments, especially in the recent past; now in the United Kingdom.

Mohamed Sannoh has the responsibility and obligation to report his findings about what he discovers, especially to the young school children in Sierra Leone, who did not witness this part of the recent history of their country, relating to the political past. Some of the facts discussed in this book are not even mentioned up till now in the education curricula, which the young school children ought to know. These are still not mentioned in their history books about what happened in their country of Sierra Leone in the recent past, because some writers and educationalists do not want to offend and step on the toes of politicians who find the facts very embarrassing, even though some of these facts could prove to justify their places in the cause of human justice. Politicians here do not tolerate revelations of their embarrassing facts, even when some of these are to rectify to avoid future occurrences of political bitterness for the benefits of their country. Politicians are to be informed of the facts that Sierra Leone belongs to these school children they are not considering in their decision makings.

Some of these school children are the politicians of tomorrow's Sierra Leone. It is just very important for them to start knowing everything about the past of their country and begin their preparations about what to encourage and what to avoid. "For the thirty-five years I have spent interacting with school children and college students in different countries of the World, I have left with the discovery that early preparations for one's country are just better than to wait till adulthood to spend dangerous political campaigns to win or rig general elections before applications of knowledge for the benefits of the country where they live. That is complete shame and disgrace not only for you but for your country as a whole including your own very biological parents. I am writing everything in this book especially when

I am not looking for a civil service job in the Sierra Leone government now and in the future.

African Politics and African Politicians' Behaviour is not leaving these embarrassing facts behind, to save the embarrassment of politicians in Sierra Leone. This will get readers into extremely enjoyable and surprising discoveries they never expected would come to light, even if they may know about some of the true facts; and for some readers, the exposures are not surprising. Mohamed Sannoh will prefer it if he is always quoted about all revelations mentioned in this book. The Devil's Advocate feet is replaced by Mohamed Sannoh's feet here in this book to cathartize his innermost feelings that have been with him for more than thirty years.

These feelings are still multiplying in different facets that are giving himself and many others sleepless nights, so that the whole world will come to know that something has gone wrong somewhere which needs all hands on deck to rectify situations for the benefits of the whole world, especially Sierra Leone and the rest of the continent of Africa.

Mohamed Sannoh, although not a practicing politician, is a member of the Sierra Leone Peoples Party (SLPP) since 1964, recruited by Pa. Juma Sei from the Eastern township of Kpaguma in the Kenema District. He is revealing in this book that African Politics is definitely a very dirty game in most African countries, but just too much in Sierra Leone. This dirty-game playing has just come to the top and started overflowing and reaching unexpected decent places. What should Sierra Leoneans do if all of us do not get up on our buttocks to say no! Enough is enough!

The following year, in 1964, a son was born to Paramount Chief Charlie Bio II of Sogbini Chiefdom of the Sherbro region as the 33rd of the 35 of his children, and that son is now President Julius Maada Bio, the current President of our country, The Republic of Sierra Leone. Mohamed Sannoh is personally pleased for Maada Bio's achievement for holding the office of the president of Sierra Leone, as he was very enthusiastic when he heard of Maada Bio's contest, and personally rallied his support wholeheartedly among the SLPP/UKI, especially in the fundraising activities, and left no stone unturned to ensure Maada Bio's success for becoming the president of Sierra Leone and representing the political party that he holds membership. As dirty political games are enjoyed by most African politicians, very few recognise and begin to see lights on the dirtiest sides and call for rectifications early before it is too late to see the light through the end of the tunnel, as Mohamed Sannoh is revealing in this book.

THE SIERRA LEONE PEOPLES' PARTY—SLPP—is THE FIRST AND OLDEST POLITICAL PARTY IN SIERRA LEONE, WHICH WAS FOUNDED BY A GROUP OF PROMINENT SIERRA LEONEANS AND HEADED BY SIR MILTON MARGAI, WHO BECAME THE FIRST PRIME MINISTER ON 27 APRIL 1964 WHEN WE GOT INDEPENDENCE FROM BRITAIN.

It is now becoming a common practice to see Chinese nationals carrying Sierra Leone Passports and engaging themselves into fighting and taking iron rods, beating Sierra Leoneans on the Leone soils on broad daylights.

This is the kind of practice that cannot be seen in the People's Republic China under the presidential leadership of President Xi Jinping. We have to beware of the Chinese invasion of our forests in our country, (Sierra Leone).

The so-called Chinese investors are also engaging in digging and mining in Cash-Crop plantations and engaged in mining our natural resources in our reserved forests with caution for soil erosion in the areas of the Kailahun District, Kenema District, Bo Districts and other parts of Sierra Leone under the security of Sierra Leone police personnel authorised by the SLPP government under the Maada Bio's administration. The Chinese investors are frequently seen on social media coverages, where they engage in depleting and cutting down trees in some parts of our forests in Sierra Leone, the only livelihood of most Sierra Leoneans, registered voters and taxpayers who have voted Maada Bio into State House as president of the Republic of Sierra Leone. All these kinds of behaviours of the Chinese people are now ridiculously circulating in the social media around the world. My main question is, "WHAT IS GOING ON?" Is Sierra Leone becoming a second phase of the West Papua community in Indonesia?

As quoted from the Holy Bible in Matthew Chapter 5:13, "You are the salt of the earth. But if the salt loses its saltiness, how can it be made salty again? It is no longer good for anything except to be thrown out and trampled by men."

Can President Julius Maada Bio please come to terms with the practical happening in Sierra Leone, before it is too late to understand that, at the moment, our country depends on him as our president to ensure that our country remains our country and not to be owned by another different national, such as the Chinese?

In September 1989, it was under Siaka Stevens' rule when Sierra Leone signed a trade agreement with China; that the latter's main exports to Sierra Leone are mechanical and electrical products, textiles and other light industrial goods, cultural and educational materials, hardware, articles for daily use, etc. At that time the leader of China was Yang Shangkun, who resigned in coincidence with the Tiananmen Square protests of 1989 after serving as Vice Chairman of the Central Military Commission between 1983 and 1993.

Although it is common for all countries to sign trade-partnership agreements as part of their diplomatic agreements with other countries of their choice, which Siaka Stevens did with genuine intentions for the benefits of Sierra Leone, Sierra Leone did not sign fighting or Agricultural and Forestry Exploitation agreements to authorise the Chinese to trot around the country beating up Sierra Leone nationals. If Chinese connection has now resulted in digging our cash-crop plantations upon which heavy amounts of sources of national income depend, it is just better for President Julius Maada Bio to call it a halt with the Chinese relationship. President Julius Maada Bio must understand that all educated Sierra Leoneans, especially those in his government and others holding top positions in the civil service, para-statals, and other private sectors of employment in Sierra Leone today, got their educational sponsorships from the Cash-Crop products, especially some of us originating from the Eastern Province of Kailahun and

Kenema Districts. Very few of these (including myself) got Sierra Leone government scholarships in their efforts for pursuing quality education that enables them to acquire the possibilities of operating today in different professional and academic capacities.

If the Chinese products have been in demand in Sierra Leone over the years, we have had enough of the fakes and we are no longer interested in dealing with the Chinese. We are not ready to fight, and we do not expect you to gradually and systematically lay the foundations of International War with China and Sierra Leone by arming the Chinese explorers with state security personnel to dig the grounds of Cash-Crop plantations by force, in Kailahun without the plantation owner's permission. These are plantations that have been developed since their arrival and introduction by the colonial governments in this country. The only sources of income for these plantation owners since the colonial occupation and through which they have been able to educate their children (including the Late Sir Milton Margai, the first Prime Minister of Sierra Leone) in this country, after which many of them have had higher education in other developed countries in the UK, US and Europe. Has President Julius Maada Bio forgotten about the importance of Cash-Crop plantation farms in Sierra Leone?

Another aspect of the Chinese exploitation ploy that has since been set in Sierra Leone is the so-called "generous gifts" that Siaka Stevens and other leaders in Sierra Leone, now including our present President Julius Maada Bio, have been accepting since the Sierra Leone-China trade deals in 1989. If you are letting us understand that you are losing your saltiness and becoming tasteless, you will just understand that there are a series of political leadership aspirants in Sierra Leone and on the waiting list, which you will be seen soon.

Why it could be very difficult to make changes in Sierra Leone politics is because the causes are deep-rooted from the top, at the State House and almost beyond the reaches of those who might have voices to shout; but some of these are echoed in this book.

President Maada Bio, one of the main disgusting areas of your administration is the free hands on the SLPP which you have let your wife, the first lady Fatima Bio, hold by behaving as a politician and taking up political engagements to represent our country in conferences abroad, when we have the appointed government ministers in your cabinets. She has not yet even been elected as an ordinary Member of Parliament—MP. She has also been referring to your Cabinet Ministers as "DOGS" in abusive manners in a public rally in the Kono-Mining talks. She is even now known to have reminded you of her political ambition when you met her first in London, UK, and now with much embarrassment she is even proven to have been challenging your presidency publicly at this twilight zone of your rule. Hence this part of her behaviour is not one of the past First Ladies of our country. We are therefore becoming uneasy with her as she has not been a true and genuine Sierra Leonean with all manners and gratitude a true Sierra Leonean woman shows to her husband of your type; hence you met in London and you becoming her fourth husband.

This book speaks to the voices of the poor and the voiceless in Africa.

There is nowhere in the whole world where developments in any sector are made successful without education, and that Sierra Leone is just too far from development if the handling of implementation of education is continuously done through political shouting. Places to visit where anyone can consider as being developed that are now enjoying the benefits of welfare status could be countries such as the United Kingdom, United States, some European States, and so on. How far are African countries, including Sierra Leone, from achieving this status where determination for human resources development will become the national dream of our African politicians, not hypocrites?

The areas of concern mainly are that almost all heads of states in Africa have either lived or visited these, they referred to as developed countries, maybe on business or during their personal developments, through education pursuits, by gaining access into educational institutions to study there.

This category of nationals in these African countries, known as African Politicians, are just behaving badly because their group works are not providing for the purposes of their employment: they are paying no attention to the development of Africa. Members of their cabinets working in political teams see the happening of the wrongs and mismanagements in action, but they keep their mouths shut so that they are not fired out of office for being so vocal in their jobs of interest.

Education is the main solution but most African Politicians do not want to hear about it, forgetting that they are in their positions because they went to school and had a taste of education. The constitution of Sierra Leone, for example, says that all members of parliament must be able to read, write, and express themselves fluently in the official language of English, accepted in the country for more than 100 years since the British colonial days, which they can do only to establish the difference from the Mende, Temne, Limba and so on, which they naturally speak as tribal languages, through basic education, which some of them are struggling with.

If politicians consider their personal needs first (which they usually do), before the needs of the nation they rule, especially during their first term of office, that behaviour will remain in the minds of the voters and will register their feelings about such leaders in the secret ballot box during the second term of office for the next General Elections that may be lying ahead of them in the country.

However, the open fact of the matter is that when anybody becomes a president in any country, especially in Africa, the perception of that person to the ordinary people including the friends they have been with changes automatically and their expectations as well become different.

One of their perceptions is that: "all the money in the country now belongs to them, and they can have access and spend the state money as when they want and upon what. Therefore, there is no black magic to enable people to read between the lines to conclude that the money that the new presidents spend on lousy wedding parties is because they have access to that state money when they (the voters) who have put him in presidential positions have nothing to eat, even out of access to clean water to drink." Most Sierra Leoneans, who are taxpayers, do not have access to clean water to drink, but the politicians can have bottled water exported from UK and USA for them to drink. This is one of the disgusting basic facts our politicians do not want anybody to pinpoint. However, it is the human right of President Julius Maada Bio to get married when and wherever he decides and to whoever he prefers among all of his numerous girlfriends, as long as he does not impinge on our Sierra Leone government's income to fulfil his personal desires, but is that truly so? Only God knows the answer.

My understanding of political practices is always problematic because problems of ruling political parties come from unexpected angles at a time. One of these angles may come from the opposition, due to eagerness to send the ruling party out of power, to give them way and clearance to occupy the political offices; as it happened in the US during the impeachment of President Donald Trump of the Republican party which was initiated by Nancy Pelosi of the Democratic party and Speaker of the House on 24 September 2019.

President Bill Clinton, the president of the Democratic Party in 1999, also suffered from impeachment embarrassment for lying under oath over the sex relations with Monica Lewinsky, who was in work placement at the White House. These impeachments did not yield against both presidents because they originated from outside their parties. These political case studies have taught me the lessons of developing the analysis that when such problems emerge from outside the boundaries of the political parties, it may not cause serious negative effects on the political parties under accusation.

But when problems occur or emerge from within the political parties themselves, especially within the ruling parties, there is cause for alarm and this may eventually result in splitting the party and ruining the efforts put into rulings from the ground. This is because when criticisms come from within the party, the criticizers know exactly what the roots of the causes of the criticism strongholds are. My understanding is that most of the origins of the causes of these problems are taken lightly and may not be serious, but these are the time bombs that are waiting to explode to take everyone by surprise.

As Mr Keketorma Sandy is now on a different list of the First Lady, let us not take it as a joke but conclude that the problem which has been knocking at the door for a long time might have entered the house of the SLPP. President Maada Bio must do something immediately.

We have Time Bombs awaiting to explode within the SLPP, the political party that I support, and the main sources of these time bombs are originating from the INNER CIRCLES of the Sierra Leone Peoples Party (SLPP). Only those who have the right eyes to see have started seeing the Time Bombs ticking. "Perhaps President Julius Maada Bio is beginning to hear the ticking of this time bomb."

The foundation stones for the destruction of the SLPP have already started from within the SLPP inner circle and these are what the opposition will be capitalising upon to catch up the SLPP voters in their main holds during the forthcoming general election in 2018.

If I am to face the main truth as SLPP member since 1964, the "First-Lady" has previously proved herself very widely, to the dislike of most SLPP voters, supporters in Sierra Leone and within the diaspora, and of course, President Julius Maada Bio has the right to take a woman into marriage if he feels single, which is why he extended his invitation to rename Fatima Jabbie into Fatima Bio in marriage. But did he do so to attract attention on Fatima Bio and at the discretion of our party, the SLPP? I think it is negative to accept childish attention to a political party, through the president's wife (First Lady).

This is much more respected when people marry once and remain husband and wife for life, as we pray for this kind of matrimony of our President Maada Bio and his wife, Fatima, because we love Maada Bio and we don't hate Fatima. When some see them taking the wrong direction, especially in the political tracks of Sierra Leone, we will shout loud, very loud and louder! Because the whole country will be the sufferers, and perhaps they will not be in the know. So, our loud shoutings are there to wake them up and remind them that the directions they might have taken are not suitable for us. That is why most Sierra Leoneans are joining with me in this book to shout loud that:

"OUR POLITICS IN OUR SIERRA LEONE IS NOT FOR SALE AND THE PRESIDENT WHO RULES FOR A TERM CANNOT BE ALLOWED TO TRANSFER OUR PRESIDENCY TO HIS WIFE/HUSBAND OR ANY OF

HIS/HER CHILDREN (AS A-WORK-HARD-FOR) FAMILY LEGACY."

If President Julius Maada Bio is not required or mandated to step down or be further elected through the democratic process as our constitutional amendment might dictate, then he will vacate respectfully from the State House office to allow another president to rule our country. This time, we will be having a new fresh, careful and respectful First Lady and may not be called Fatima, although we still remain with the appreciate of Fatima Jabbie-Bio and remember her as the one-time First Lady.

Out of curiosity to know about some psychological facts about our first lady, I don't want to live on assumptions in my mind, applicable to all human beings, which has tickled my mindset recently. These questions have come up because of testing the following human theories observed about Mrs Fatima Bio, the wife of President Julius Maada Bio. Let me explain here just a very few psychological discoveries I have made about human nature:

i. Persona: The personality that a person adopts and presents to other people.

ii. Disorder: (i) A state of untidiness and disorganised

iii. (ii) Public violence or rioting (iii) An illness

iv. Mental Illness: Any of various disorders in which a person's thoughts, emotions, or behaviour are so abnormal as to cause suffering to himself or herself or other people.

v. Persona Disorder: The earlier stages of mental illness which cause people to behave disorderly in public through expressions in thoughts and behaviours. Persona disorder is just the first earlier stage where mental health medical professionals begin to discover about mental health patients in their processes of diagnoses. The sufferers experience this in public without noticing, but sometimes as in the pretext being humorous.

Now, when Mrs Fatima Bio attended the inauguration of the Chairman of the SLPP-UK/I some time ago in London, she went over the top and referred to all PhD holders as the most stupid fools on earth, because these are the people who know nothing about politics and always end up shooting their legs whenever they hold guns to shoot. She made this statement on the SLPP political platform as a Guest of Honour (the wife of the President of Sierra Leone, representing the SLPP). At the same time this president is trotting the world and pleading to highly educated Sierra Leoneans in the diaspora to join his cabinet to shape the dismantled condition he is inheriting in our Sierra Leone. Are those high-calibre educated professionals, such as Dr. David Moinina Sengheh, the former Minister of Education and now the First Minister of the cabinet, and many other highly educated Sierra Leoneans, very stupid, just useless, and taking part in the politics of Sierra Leone?

These are the tainted records of Mrs Fatima Jabbie-Bio which she has planted on the political platform of Sierra Leone that will never go unnoticed.

At this point in time in our country, can anyone consider that statement from Mrs Fatima Bio as a sense of humour comment or disrespect for people like us who are education enthusiasts, left Sierra Leone for years in search of education to the highest level, to return home to make good contributions at professional as well as academic stages in Sierra Leone? I would just like to advise President Julius Maada Bio to please consider assisting his lovely Mrs Fatima Bio for medical testing to find out exactly her mental health condition before it is just too late, because all PhD holders in London and all over the world who might have heard that statement from Mrs Fatima Bio are very saddened and here again, she must make a very open apology for her stinky behaviour. If this is one of her ploys and tactics to destroy SLPP, where was she at the establishment of our political party in 1951?

If she is looking for someone to give her a public disgraceful mouth-washing, let her be assured that there are SLPP members who will provide her with that favour if she does not behave with decency in future, especially on the SLPP platforms in any country, even including The Gambia. The SLPP Political party is not a toy for her to just play with as she likes. "Gambian nationals are our friends and our long-distance relatives." Wide rumours from reliable sources escalated that the SLPP voters were planning to withhold their votes because the President's wife has mouth-washed them publicly on different occasions because she does not have respect for them. The SLPP as a political party in Sierra Leone is seriously against such misbehaviour to members. What has President Maada Bio got to say about this?

President Julius Maada Bio must understand that SLPP members are tired of the rudeness of his wife, and at any time she displays that kind of rudeness on the SLPP political platform in any of the SLPP meetings. Does she realise now that the "cocoa roast" singing saga was just a test case which can be devastatingly regretted over?

President Julius Maada Bio must also know that we love the Sierra Leone Peoples Party (SLPP) far more than him and his wife, and there are so many other Sierra Leoneans who are qualified enough to hold the office of the President of Sierra Leone but not Fatima in the manner in which she is moving. She is trying to destroy our political party—(SLPP)—and we will not allow her to do so. She must go through the procedure and she must at first work hard to understand this.

As much as we may like President Maada Bio's wife, the First Lady Fatima Jabbie-Bio, we will not allow her to destroy our lives in Sierra Leone to migrate to live in the UK, to take advantage of her dual nationality status.

"We are very nationalistic about our political presidency and we will not consider any other national to hold the office of president in our country. Those who will be hailing politicians with a small sense of foreign connections on their nationalities will be after sucking money out of them, just to disappoint them at the ballot box in the polling booth through democratic process of—one man, one vote—known to the voters themselves alone."

The majority of voters for the SLPP value their personal respects and dignities more than any other gift anyone can give to them. This is Sierra Leone, and our country is not called The Gambia, where Mrs Fatima Bio originates. The SLPP voters are beginning to come to terms that this "First Lady" of Maada Bio is not in their political interest, because of stepping down on their respects and dignities. Secondly, the country elected one president in Sierra Leone in the 2018 General Elections and not two, (including his wife). This "First Lady" connotation is just very new in the Sierra Leone politics which needs to be structured properly for the understanding of the native voters who are in majority and to check the behavioural aspects and connections of the president's wife.

Mrs Fatima Bio is a wife only of President Julius Maada Bio and not for the whole country. All married women in Sierra Leone are RESPECTED FIRST LADIES of their husbands. They are not First Ladies for the whole country. Voters for SLPP want to see their president working in a respectable manner and not dedicating all public activities to his wife (who is not a politician) who is trotting villages in political capacity as First Lady of the state. A First Lady political title is not constituted in our style of politics or constitution in Sierra Leone. We want to remain Sierra Leoneans with all assurances and dignities and not in a plagiarised decorated style. Those who admire American style should go and live there but not in our Sierra Leone. We are a civilised, respected and educated nation. Don't ever underrate a man you may come across in a village dressed as a farmer. He might have been a university graduate from a country that you don't expect. They are well educated and know more than you. They are in the bush conditions that you see them because they are Sierra Leoneans. Is there any problem with that?

This is not our style of politics in Sierra Leone and we elected only one president and not his wife. We have a Vice President in the personality of Mohamed Julde Jalloh.

This is the man we prefer seeing on the political platform, in assistance to President Julius Maada Bio because he is collecting monthly salaries and other state benefits for holding the office of the Vice President of Sierra Leone, and I think he should be given the chance to do his work properly and to gain the relevant experience he needs and that he will confidently add to his Curriculum Vitae (CV). If President Maada Bio's hands are full, we have the Vice President Dr Mohamed Julde Jalloh, and why should he not be engaged rather than Fatima Bio? Has our Vice President become redundant now or has he been replaced with Mrs. Fatima Bio, the wife of President Julius Maada Bio? Is Mrs Fatima Bio now the new Vice President of Sierra Leone? The SLPP is not known as a political party that sacks the Vice President and replaces him with another politician unconstitutionally. So why now is the force?

Let me educate all Sierra Leoneans that the title of "First Lady" is of American origin, meaning the wife of the President. Why should this be glorified in Sierra Leone, which is a different African state?

Why is this type of 'plagiarism' in the eyes of High Calibre Academics in Sierra Leone not condemned but allowed to become additional to our styles of politics? Have the Academics of Sierra Leone pledged or sacrificed their academic status to politics? This uneasy political show has no meaning and it is bringing down SLPP within the SLPP voters because the SLPP is a political party, not "a woman show business club."

Recently, the wife of the president, Mrs Fatima Bio, is trotting on social media with cries that people have poisoned and killed her brother (Marabou), who was a footballer playing for East End Lions in Freetown. She is saying that his brother's drink was (spiked) poisoned by someone when they went into a warehouse for a drink. In my attempt to educate Mrs Fatima Bio (President Julius Maada Bio's First Lady), I would just let her understand that Sierra Leone has been formally declared as a Christian Country since 1792. Christianity was brought to Sierra Leone by the Nova Scotian Settlers when they founded the Colony of Sierra Leone in March 1792.

The Constitution provides for freedom of religion, and the Government generally respected this right in practice. Intermarriage between Muslims and Christians is common, and that is just one of the commonalities that gave her the opportunity that propelled her marriage to a Christian husband in the person of Julius Maada Bio, now the President of the Government of Sierra Leone. That statement has no proof and it is just very offensive to the whole of the Sierra Leone community both at home and in the rest of the Diasporas in the world. Sierra Leoneans don't kill people just like that, except in self-defence. Additionally, Christians are, however, very tolerant to Muslims in Sierra Leone more than any other country in the world because Christians in this country believe in accepting and respecting all human beings of the world because they are all created by the Almighty God who came and lived in the world as human being in the person of Jesus Christ. Muslims in Sierra Leone are considered by Christians as their fellow human beings, whom they love and sincerely cherish as equal members of their human family in this lovely beautiful country. That is why she was not killed when she was born here, originating from The Gambia.

This is what Jesus Christ told his followers, including all Christians in Sierra Leone. We will never tolerate religious hate among us in our country. Therefore, we do not accept Mrs Fatima Bio's disrespectful and spiky comments of Sierra Leoneans killing her brother, without proving such hateful accusations. Furthermore, this country is just one of the safest places on the planet earth that accommodates all nationalities from different parts of the globe. She is just one of the living experiences of this statement when her father, Mr Umar Jabbie, arrived in this country in search of diamond wealth from The Gambia, where he got married to a Sierra Leonean lady in the person of Tigidankay, of Kono tribe and gave birth to her on 27 November 1980.

She is one of the privileged few who have been benefiting from the humanity and generosity of Sierra Leone where she has found President Julius Maada Bio, president of the Republic of the country who is accepting her as her FOURTH HUSBAND.

Despite our bitter experience of ten years of civil war from 23 March 1991 – 18 January 2002, Sierra Leone still remains a country with high value of human dignity, and spiking Marabou's drink with poison, as Mrs Fatima Bio is disseminating (without autopsy justification) on social media, is classed as being ungrateful and at the extreme end of narcissism which Sierra Leoneans do not expect, despite her interests in attention seeking. This is becoming very offensive as it is considered as one of her ploys to destroy our political party of Sierra Leone Peoples Party (SLPP).

All of us in Sierra Leone, both home and in the diaspora, are in sympathy with her bereavement of her brother, Marabou, especially East End Lions Football Club Members in Freetown. This is a very strong social club where people meet, both players and the general public, including members, to enjoy themselves. Here at the East End Lions Football Club, the Young and the Old always seize the opportunities to meet, drink, enjoy, laugh, provoke, mock each other, reminisce about the good old days, and catch-up with the new fresh booties of the environment.

Secondly, Mrs Fatima Bio must understand that all of us on earth are liable to die one day and none of us know the time when individual death will knock at one's door.

If your brother's time has arrived recently without his notice, this is just the usual practice of all human life, regardless of being a Muslim. We all sympathise with your bereavement, but blaming anyone for having done this without autopsy results is not Sierra Leonean style of behaviour, and we condemn these comments you are making on social media which demand a very open apology to the public of Sierra Leone and the East End Lions Football Club.

For your information, Sierra Leone is a civilized country in a civilized society and killing people is not our habit; perhaps this is normal in The Gambia.

Mrs Fatima Bio is not a politician and she is not the President of Sierra Leone. If her imagination about herself has gone too far beyond her imagination, myself and some other members of the SLPP are ready to make our voices heard far and wide, and to advise President Julius Maada Bio to have a one-to-one conversation with his wife, whose love he is putting above the SLPP's interest. Is President Julius Maada Bio in the State House to show love to his wife or to perform his presidential duties? Does President Julius Maada Bio love his wife in his capacity as the President of Sierra Leone, elected by the political party of the Sierra Leone Peoples Party (SLPP) or the country of Sierra Leone? This LOVE MAKING SHOW-OFF is not part of our politics in Sierra Leone and we do not like it. It is not in the interest of Sierra Leone as a country and Sierra Leone Peoples Party (SLPP) as a political party.

SLPP is not a play toy and we are no longer ready to accept any type of ridiculous mouth washing show-off from our "First Lady" in Sierra Leone, of the poor people in our villages.

We want them to rest in peace and we believe that President Julius Maada Bio is ready to provide them with this peace, which the late President Tejan Kabbah founded earlier; otherwise, we are ready to change our position as a result of his wife.

We are all advised to learn from the Donald Trump and Joe Biden election of 2020 in America that it is not just enough to say that it is automatic for an incumbent presidential candidate to win.

Increase of Democratic Politics is rapidly on the rise all over the world, and the politics of Sierra Leone cannot be exempted.

The mistake that brought Donald Trump the down position in the 2020 election in America was when he earlier on looked down upon and referred to Africa as a "Sheet-Hole" country. That connotation did not go down well in the whole world, especially in Africa, and there is no country that does not want African countries diplomatic connection. Former US President Donald Trump of the Republican Party left a legacy that cannot be easily erased. He left a legacy of racial divide, discrimination, disrespectfulness of the Black people in America and Africa as a whole.

The Council of Churches in Sierra Leone (CCSL)

The Council of Churches in Sierra Leone (CCSL) is an umbrella organisation of seventeen member churches and ten affiliates. Speaking with a united voice, it promotes peace, justice and development. Its strength is being deeply rooted in the communities it serves.

The existence of this organisation is well known to the government of Sierra Leone, since its foundation in 1924 with the following mission statement:

"We as a Council of Churches in Sierra Leone affirm our belief in the one-eternal God, Creator and Lord of the world:

Father, Son and Holy Spirit, who governs all things according to the purpose of his will. He has been calling out from the world a people for himself, and sending his people back into the world to be his servants and witnesses, for the extension of his kingdom, the building of Christ's body and the glory of his name.

The Council of Churches in Sierra Leone is the covenant enhancing the unity of our member churches on the basis of partnership and a guide as to how we undertake our mission."

It is within the initiatives of the Government of Sierra Leone to take decisions in the interests of the people of the country of Sierra Leone.

However, if any of the government's decisions are for the interest of the people of Sierra Leone, it will be very necessary to pre-inform or have an emergency meeting with The Council of Churches before effecting that decision, simply in the interest of the people of Sierra Leone, and this would have propelled respected respects and appreciations for the roles that the CCSL is playing among the people of Sierra Leone.

The government's decision that came from the President's office of President Julius Maada Bio is to stop all Christian worship in all churches in the country, in preparation to avoid an outbreak of the Corona Virus Pandemic in the country.

Social media communications received directly by UK listeners reveal that the CCSL is not taking this immediate close down action lightly because they were unprepared as to what to tell their congregations, especially when such should always have a uniform information that could have been agreed upon by the CCSL administration. The CCSL immediately released their concern to the President and asked him to withdraw the statement with immediate effect. The president has written back that he will be reviewing the situation periodically in future.

Now, the CCSL is neither a political organisation nor a dictating force to tell the government what to do or what not to do; but putting the CCSL in such embarrassing situations is considered as being tantamount to discrediting the CCSL organisation.

Can anyone just try to ask whether President Julius Maada Bio's action is just because he is working on a personal agenda to stimulate satisfaction to his wife Mrs Fatima Bio because she is not a Christian but a Muslim by faith? It would appear that President Julius Maada Bio is taking national matters into his personal bedroom, which is just mismatching and mixing up what to do and what not to do.

Some analysts are coming up with different conclusions that the best solution is to ask President Julius Maada Bio to resign from the State House Office respectfully and give the Head of State position to another SLPP Flag-Bearer, so that he will have enough time to spend with his newly married wife, Mrs Fatima Bio of The Gambia origin and keep her happy, hence this State Leadership is making it difficult for him to fulfil his wife's happiness.

It is his responsibility to make his wife happy so that they will remain as a happily married couple for the rest of their lives that lie ahead. This wife has openly said on the World social media platform that "she loves President Julius Maada Bio so much that she is ready to do anything for him to make him happy." What else would anyone like to hear from any of them if we are to face the truth? They are just human beings like any of us created by the Almighty God and let us treat them very fairly. However, the SLPP Delegates Conference will decide.

The best of the democratic practice of modern politics was demonstrated and practiced by F.W. DeKlerk, who ruled South Africa from 1989 to 1994. This legacy is effected because he inherited a racist regime of White Supremacy in the black majority country in Africa where the black people were not allowed and deprived of certain privileges of the country because they were black—the colour of their skins. Africans were not even given the privileges of voting in their own country of birth because of this reason. Shamelessly, the fake white leaders referred to their system as the White Minority Rule of democracy.

If it comes to the point of boycotting our votes for SLPP in Sierra Leone during the forthcoming election, this could be an alarm call to President Julius Maada Bio that all members and voters of the SLPP prefer to be Highly Respected than allowing his wife to trot around the country abusing villagers as she is presently doing. We are very highly civilised people and we do not look down on our feet but up to the sky because that is where the Almighty God lives.

F.W. DeKlerk saw that this kind of political atmosphere was not genuine and not free and fair to the human race in which all human beings were required to live. He, being a white man, allowed black people to demonstrate against white rules and allowed free and fair elections in which all South Africans were allowed to vote (for the first time), which brought Nelson Mandela, the first black president, to power.

He ruled for only one term of office "from 10 May 1994 to 14 June 1999."

When Nelson Mandela became president of South Africa on 10 May 1994, he turned away from political retaliation against the previous white leadership under the Apartheid.

This is the education aspect that when one forgives those who cause harm to them, they will live in peace with each other, because the world in which we live is for all human beings being black or white or mixed. President Nelson Mandela faced the fact that there would have been no peace in South Africa if he was to exercise "political powers" against white people there when he became President of that country in 1994. Instead, he gave blanket amnesty freedom to all South Africans through the Truth and Reconciliation that he established.

All Politicians in African countries must learn from these examples of African Politics and African Politicians Behaviour, and this was what our Late President Ahmad Tejan Kabbah of the Sierra Leone Peoples Party (SLPP) learned from and applied when he became president on 29 March 1996 from the United Nations. May his soul rest in

Great Perfect Peace for enhancing peace for Sierra Leone after the Civil War from 23 March to 18 January 1992.

“President Kabbah promised peace, and he delivered peace for Sierra Leone.”

EDUCATION DATELINES IN SIERRA LEONE
From: 1961- To: 2025

(1). The Past

Introduction

Although this paper seeks to focus on investigating the historical background of primary and secondary school settings in Sierra Leone after independence from Britain in 1961 to 2025, some attempts are made to explain the historical past as far back as 1787, when the formal system of education started in this West African state at the beginning of British colonial occupation.
The West African Secondary School Certificate Examination (WASSCE), administered by the West African Examinations Council (WAEC), is suffering from secondary/high school level examination malpractices such as examination leakages, according to newspaper reports—such as 29-05-2019 - 03:05:56 am of Graphic.com, Ghana Web 29 May 2019, Ghana Web (Crimes and Punishment) of 7 June 2019, Church of Pentecost 29 May 2019, and finally, Ibrahim P. Sheriff, who reiterated that "The quality of education in Sierra Leone over the past decades has continued to degenerate to the point where the trend seriously undermines the human capacity development of the country's populace. Key to the degeneration is how much almost every facet of Sierra Leonean society participates in examination malpractices—pupils, students, teachers,

examination officers, the public examining body of the West African Examinations Council (WAEC), parents, police, and so on," as explained on 18 July 2019 by The Patriotic Vanguard. The examination system is heavily penetrated, shamelessly, by politicians, causing credible post-secondary educational institutions, including most employers, to turn their backs on this qualification, although still reluctant to do so, as WAEC remains the only yardstick of measurement for educational assessments at foundational levels in schools.

With all these revelations, one can see that the external school examination system throughout West Africa, including Sierra Leone, is seriously damaged and far below recognition within educational circles, particularly with reference to gaining admission into highly developed post-secondary educational institutions internationally. As my research into educational standards in Sierra Leone reveals in this book, political unsettlement, mismanagement, corruption, political disagreements that resulted in eleven years of civil war, and many other issues such as human rights violations are held responsible for breaking this national precious gold—EDUCATION—into pieces.

Corruption resulting in examination malpractices, according to plain facts, is encouraged by the governments of countries benefiting from WAEC examinations because education workers in primary and secondary schools are paid far less than the workers they put into education daily. However, the present government of the SLPP is continuously engaged in talks to get teachers to relax a bit, which has still left the few educated government employees open to many temptations to obtain money for the sustenance of their meagre salaries to make ends meet. The previous APC left the nation in serious disarray and disagreement among its higher ranks, which compulsorily forced the party leader to plead for access out of the country to Nigeria when the Sierra Leone court charged him with a criminal offence, just as it would anyone else in the country. Is he still in Nigeria pleading to return home?

Perhaps the only solution to solving examination malpractices is to design and establish "Leakage-Free External Examinations" that will service primary and secondary schools; otherwise, the future of our children is heading to doom and to the pleasure of politicians who have the power to obtain money to send their own children to schools in developed countries, leaving poor, talented children to suffer. For example, Ernest Bai Koroma, president of the APC government, had his two daughters educated in London, UK, while many other talented children are left to scramble for education in underdeveloped institutions. Such problems can only be solved when children go to school in this country free of charge, as the current SLPP government under President Julius Maada Bio is encouraged to do.

1816: Brief Historical Background of Education in Sierra Leone:

Sierra Leone has experienced the benefits of educational leadership in the sub-Saharan region of Africa under the description of "The Athens of West Africa," Paraka Jr. J.D. (2003), as far as the history of education in that region can explain. Especially when the British government and the Church Missionary Society (CMS) agreed in 1816 (www.cambridge.org/core/journals/history-in-africa) to build churches, schools, and parsonages in Sierra Leone and for the CMS to staff villages with ministers and schoolmasters.

The same source reveals that by 1824, some 2,460 children were receiving education in the colony schools, according to an internet report. CMS provision was very high. Since Sierra Leone was and still is a multi-religious society before the arrival of colonial masters, there was little conflict between locals and CMS missionaries.

Since CMS's main mission was to spread Christianity through the children they contacted, and because these children came from different religious homes, they were not very comfortable with children who were reluctant to accept Christianity.

Therefore, sour relationships were experienced—interpreted as CMS missionaries being discriminatory against those of other religions—although this may not have been the case. As the report later explains about the confusion, the Sierra Leonean community complained succinctly that the CMS education system was "too bookish" for their children to comprehend, leading to a form of civil disobedience by the locals—the first strike in Sierra Leone—which the locals did not obey under their then British colonial masters.

Earlier Styles of Education in Sierra Leone before Colonisation in 1787:

British colonisation of Sierra Leone is recorded to have started in 1787.

Since the British administration bade "Good-Bye" to Sierra Leone after independence on 27 April 1961, the country has not experienced educational success that benefits its existing talents for many reasons.

British colonial occupation in Sierra Leone lasted for 174 years (1787–1961). This was a long time under the colony's education system, sending natural provisions of gold and diamonds to the UK for the Queen's possession, mostly stored in the vaults of the Bank of England. The local people were already practising their own system of learning in their own ways before the British arrived and imposed a formal education system using letters of the alphabet. This introduction of the western style education system required people to study in English, a new language which was quite foreign. This was an additional burden on the people, which was not easy to cope with, but with hard determination, they did it.

Why did the British not learn and adopt any of the Sierra Leonean indigenous languages into the official language of communication for education and administrative purposes? Were they not ready to learn African languages, dress, and behave like Africans do? Why did they not open local language learning centres to provide tuition in Mende, Temne, Limba, and so on, if they needed to learn from nationals in their own country? Instead, English became the official language for communication, education, and administration in Sierra Leone, the West African nation. This part of education history was already cautioned by E. S. Sawyer at McGill University, Canada.

1787—The Commencement of the British Colonial Experience—Start of the Former System:

The year 1787 was when formal education started in Sierra Leone using the alphabet of the English language as the medium of communication. This was so because colonial masters at this time spoke none of the indigenous languages of Sierra Leone. The British heavily depended on sign languages, possibly as strong pillars in general communications with locals, followed by thorough explanations.

1827: Pacesetting of Educational Standards in Sub-Saharan Africa:

Sierra Leone was the first country in sub-Saharan Africa to establish a western-style education system through the establishment of Fourah Bay College (FBC) on 18 February 1827, before Conservative MP William Wilberforce's proposal "to end slavery" came to approval by the British Parliament in England, ending slavery in 1833. It took America another thirty years to end this inhuman trade in 1863 through a constitutional amendment. Slavery was so entrenched in the American state of Texas that it took authorities there another ten years to accept and get rid of treating Black people as slaves.

To this day, some American whites struggle with ridding slavery because they have come to believe the practice is a strong pillar of the American economy. Through slavery, they enjoy free labor without paying for it. This causes ongoing problems for Black Americans, who are in America because they were born there, not by choice. Their forefathers and ancestors were captured from Africa as slaves and shipped to American slave markets.

They worked hard under flogging, pain, and sometimes death, without seeing their African homelands, to make America what it is today, including the construction of the White House. They were even forced to accept the identities and names given by slave masters, such as Kinta Kunte, captured in Juffreh village in The Gambia, West Africa, near Sierra Leone; Alex Haley explained in Roots (1997). Kunta Kinteh was forced to accept the name "Toby" under merciless beatings and torture. Today, whites who inflicted such suffering do not want to see these people in America, where those born and bred know no other home. This could be called a "shithole" country, not any African country.

The treatment of Black people in America is profoundly evil. If in the position of Donald Trump, calling himself the current president of America (as of September 2020), one would think carefully before using nasty comments referring to some countries in Africa as a "shithole country."

After all, what America has done to Africa (through racial discrimination) has contributed to Africa's underdevelopment and predicaments today because of American exploitation. If ethical judgment is needed, which country deserves the label "shithole"—America or Africa?

Donald Trump failed to realize Sierra Leone is not among countries he described as "shithole." After abolition of slavery on 18 December 1865, the province of freedom was founded in 1787. This province formed the city of Sierra Leone, called Freetown, founded on 11 March 1792.

It was declared that all slaves who found themselves in Freetown were no longer slaves but free men. Thus, Sierra Leone does not fit Donald Trump's description of African countries. If he thinks so, he holds a profound misconception and political bluff.

He has misconceived Africa profoundly, showing immoral and unethical behavior. He has sown political discord unlikely to germinate on American soil, perhaps only on his German ancestral soil. A politician without insight cannot see the truth but only incites trouble. Such a person is Donald J. Trump of the USA.

Slavery is the backbone of America. America is the worst place on Earth for human dwellings, where satanic behavior condemned by God is enjoyed.

As of 7 October 2020, the American white racist policeman who killed George Floyd by pressing his knee on Floyd's neck to death in Minnesota on 25 May 2020 (igniting Black Lives Matter protests) was released from prison on bail of $1 million, as BBC news announced. Between May and October is less than five months, and this man of evil was freed to mingle with the community. What does this say about the American system? White racists go to prison holidays for horrendous crimes as long as they can pay bail, with President Trump's endorsement. So, which country is the "shithole"—the USA or any African country? Mr. Floyd's funeral was held at Fountain of Praise Church in Houston, Texas, on 9 June 2020, attended by Joe Biden, former Vice President under Barack Obama, where Floyd was laid to rest peacefully.

As long as Donald Trump called Africa "a shithole community," he has brought calamity to the United States as long as he stays in power. American voters will decide, understanding that the US is what it is because of slavery's forced extraction of human resources from Africa. This slavery will remain part of African history education lessons in Sierra Leone and throughout Africa.

At this point, I would like to communicate to Donald Trump that Sierra Leone is still a place of safe haven where people such as Black Americans, whose forefathers once suffered from slavery and whose descendants now suffer from inhuman treatments of slavery in different forms—as seen in the cases of George Floyd, Breonna Taylor, and many others who rose to Black Lives Matter protests—originate, and he is not a president acting in the interest of America.

Why was America not selected as a safe haven for freedom for slaves? This is because America itself has been a "shithole" country since those days, unsuitable for human existence, and that situation continues today. Is Donald Trump expecting the Almighty God to take action on America as happened to Sodom and Gomorrah, as described in the Holy Bible (Genesis 18:20)?

What disgusts me about that comment is that most Black people in America today are descendants of Sierra Leoneans. Their forefathers were captured as slaves in Sierra Leone by evil slave traders such as John Hawkins, a slave trader along the West African coast in the 1590s. He later invested his slavery income into education, which led to the establishment of John Hawkins University in Maryland, Baltimore in 1876. This system of slave income money laundering continues to generate enormous income for the American economy. Is that not "a shithole country"?

My personal opinion about Donald Trump, although I respect all presidents of America, is that he might share joint DNA with Nazis in Germany or the KKK, which explains his lack of regard for humanity on God's planet Earth, should a scientific laboratory test be conducted on him. He is not even a Christian but used the Christian community in the November 2016 election. Having now "uncovered his true skin," he is even shy to knock on any church doors in the USA. What he is embarking on publicly is rubbing shoulders with President Benjamin Netanyahu of Israel, intending to win votes from the Jewish community in America. The Jewish people are not stupid but very clever, as he will live to see.

Donald Trump must understand that people who hide behind their fingers are always caught by their ears and brought forward to discipline for telling lies. This is what American voters are going to show him in the 9 November 2020 presidential election in the

USA. He will never smell the White House again and should not bother running in future elections because he is a lifelong failure. Soon after his defeat, perpetual lights will begin to shine on his falsifications that may eventually lead him to prison.

This will make him understand that the Almighty God is always awake to look after those wrongfully treated by authorities such as Donald Trump, who think they have power in their hands and can mistreat Black people as much as they want.

FBC became a degree-granting institution when it established a linkage with Durham University in the UK in 1876. This collaboration created international educational opportunities for many Africans in the region to take advantage of studying there and obtain British degrees from Durham University.

As our neighboring countries under the Sahara once looked up to Sierra Leone as the pacesetter of educational standards in the sub-region, this dream can only become reality now with a 'system change—the political system' starting from the educational foundation stages in primary and secondary schools.

As the politics of Sierra Leone has already ruined the education system for thirty-six (36) years under the All-Peoples Congress (APC) political party regimes, led by Siaka Stevens, Joseph Saidu Momoh, and Ernest Bai Koroma. The APC policy towards education is that "education should not be a priority for government expenditure for the country". Those who feel that education is a necessity should either go to other countries or send their children to countries where good education is available. Practically, APC politicians, such as former President Ernest Bai Koroma, have had their children educated in the UK, USA, and other countries, leaving poor, talented children competing for places where there are outdated and ruined facilities. The APC government refused to accept that even those countries now referred to as developed nations, including Britain, were some years ago far behind Sierra Leone. They overcame backwardness only through education. This is the cry of many Sierra Leonean lovers, which President Julious Maada Bio listened to as a politician and not with the country's natural riches in his overseas bank account, saved for his future retirement. This is absolutely morally wrong to humanity in any country, under any government.

Therefore, with a focus on education, I would like to reiterate what led to the decline in educational standards in primary and secondary schools in Sierra Leone since its independence from Britain in 1961.

> The difference between these two institutions, established in 1876 is that the John Hawkins University was born out of evil practices (Slavery) in America and the Fourah Bay College (University of Sierra Leone) was born out of Christianity (Holy Spirit) by the Church Missionary Society (CMS) from the United Kingdom, two years later after the Wesleyan Mission founded the Methodist Boys' High School on 26 April 1874.

THE COLLAPSE OF EDUCATIONAL STANDARDS IN BASIC EDUCATION IN SIERRA LEONE: (revisiting 1827-1849)

According to a Sierra Leonean migrant in Canada, Mr. A. K. Kamara, his report published in Patrioticvanguard.com in 2013 started with the following comments:

"Western education was introduced into Sierra Leone and the rest of British West Africa by the Church Missionary Society (CMS) in the early 19th century, with Sierra Leone leading the way in this direction". He continued with his commentary that "Having led the way in Western education in West Africa, one would imagine that Sierra Leone should by now be the best and the leader of other Anglophone countries in the sub-region; they should be looking up to Sierra Leone as the model for educational accomplishments. Unfortunately, this has not been the case. Educationally, our country is at the tail end today. The first university institution in West Africa, Fourah Bay College, The Athens of West Africa, interestingly started in 1827 without a single secondary school either in Sierra Leone or West Africa. It was eighteen years later that the very first secondary school for boys, the CMS Grammar, was opened in 1845 in Freetown, and four years later another for girls, the Annie Walsh Memorial School, was started in 1849."

Primary school education, scheduled during the colonial days, was meant to run for eight years duration at two levels.

The first level was class one and class two (2 years). Upon completion of that level, the next level of primary education was the standard classes: standard one to standard six (6 years). At the completion of standard six, students were prepared to take their first external examination called the "Common Entrance Examination (CEE)" for entry into secondary schools.

In total, 2 years in classes 1 & 2 and 6 years from standard 1 to standard 6 sum up to 8 solid years (2+6=8) in primary school. These years were considered very solid because they were spent on educational foundations, a very important stage in a learner's life.

There were no multiple-choice questions in the common entrance examination, and the Arithmetic and English exams in those days were really of a very high standard that required pupils to study hard in their preparations. The teachers were actual colonial teachers trained by the colonial masters from Britain.

1961: Independence from Britain

The Sierra Leone Peoples Party (SLPP), formed in 1951, was the first political party in Sierra Leone with the first Prime Minister, Sir Milton Margai, after independence from Britain. When Sierra Leone became independent in 1961, the then Prime Minister greeted the event with the assertion, 'Sierra Leone will become a model state.' Since then, however, the country has experienced increasing corruption and authoritarianism, rigged elections, and a series of coups. Political change has been, apparently, both dramatic and deleterious according to Christopher Allen of Nuffield College at Oxford (2019). The education system of the country was up to date when the British left after independence in 1961.

An opposition party, the All Peoples Congress (APC), was founded in 1960 and became the first opposition political party in the country. The APC won the general elections in 1968 and governed from that year to 1992 and again from 2012 to March 2018 (a total of 30 years of APC rule in Sierra Leone). During this period, the education system plummeted below the standard of expectations.

The founder of the APC political party, Siaka Stevens, was a retired policeman who did not have or recognize the value of educational qualifications and expressed special dislike for educational institutions including Fourah Bay College, now a constituent college of the University of Sierra Leone. The usual educational support for primary and secondary schools started disappearing, and the multiplication of ghost teachers began resulting in the misappropriation of funds in the government treasury. Another social disadvantage created by the APC political party was the lack of promotion of educational necessity in the Northern Province in Sierra Leone, with the understanding that when people are educated there, they will rise against him and kick him out of power. Today, the people in these communities are left with great bitterness for not being educated.

The common entrance examination was standardized to either pass or fail, and those who failed were left with no alternative but to repeat the class standard and sit the examination again to gain a pass grade to enter a secondary school of choice.

CHANGE OF GOVERNMENT AND THE EFFECTS OF POLITICS ON EDUCATION:

1951: The formation of the Sierra Leone Peoples Party (SLPP)

The first and oldest political party in Sierra Leone, known as the Sierra Leone Peoples Party (SLPP), was established in 1951 before independence. Ten years later, in 1961, when the country was a member of the British Commonwealth of Nations under the leadership of the first Prime Minister Sir Milton Margai.

1952: The West African Examinations Council:

"Established in 1952 as an examining board to determine the examinations required in the public interest in the English-speaking West African countries, to conduct the examinations, and to award certificates comparable to those of equivalent examining authorities internationally." The West African Examinations Council (WAEC) has contributed to education in Anglophonic countries of West Africa (Ghana, Nigeria, Sierra Leone, Liberia, and The Gambia), with the number of examinations they have coordinated and certificates they have issued." (www.google.com/search?safe=strict&source=)

This examinations council started with sound reliability for measuring educational standards in the primary and secondary school education sector under the British colonial era in Sierra Leone, which continued through independence in 1961 and beyond up to this time in 2019.

Since 1952 to 2019, which is now 67 years by my calculation, no other external examining body addressing education issues in the categories of

primary and secondary schools' examinations and assessment has been established. It appears that the government of Sierra Leone has either forgotten the importance of a solid educational foundation or perhaps totally neglected these areas.

During another research I completed about the number of secondary schools in the North, South, and Eastern provinces in Sierra Leone for one of my postgraduate qualifications MA (Education) completed at Plymouth Marjon University in Cornwall, I was unable to discover any existing document about curriculum review of public examinations of the West African Examinations Council (WAEC) that are still going on in Sierra Leone, which I suggest might have been destroyed during the civil war or might have gone out of date and deliberately destroyed because it is not good for purpose.

1962: Senior Primary (SP-1) and (SP-2) added:

At the start of the academic school year 1962, two more years of Senior Primary (SP-1) and Senior Primary (SP-2) were added to the primary years' level. The purpose was to make proper provisions for the preparation of children before moving into secondary schools, to lower the rate of failure among school children, and to motivate them to stick to education until they finish secondary school or enter the university stage of education.

Therefore, the addition of the third layer of SP-1 and SP-2 made a total of ten years of part-1, the education foundation years in primary school. Although parents, especially in the provinces, had very high regard for educational value, the Creoles (descendants of the free slaves who live in Freetown) came to realize that educational qualification was the only source of survival requiring them to earn a living through employment either in the civil service or private companies that started springing up through investments of individuals.

The Creole fellows came to notice that they didn't have family possessions such as

plantations for agriculture; hence, originating from free slaves and finding themselves in freedom out of the predicament of slavery in Freetown was God's given chance for them to progress in life, live easily, and earn money to buy houses, cars, clothes, have beautiful wives, and live in comfort through education only, and nothing else.

Even today, education is the only way through which the Creole people survive in Sierra Leone. They are desperate to be given the right to buy land in provincial areas, but the political constitution has not made provisions for permanent ownership of land possessions because they are always engaged in farming and plantations to justify ownership differently from farming.

Therefore, the community land tenure system ownership is practiced, which they occupy rotationally on a first-come-first-served basis through understanding and negotiations between families. Although the Creoles are trying very hard to penetrate this venture, the provincials have come to realize that it will only be in the Creole-man's own interests. The Creole people's interest is to have the right to sell their land documents to millionaires living in America

who will only be interested in digging for natural resources to take to America, leaving the land unusable for farming, as has been done in most areas in the Kono district. This kind of education is now teaching most communities in the provinces about their land ownership, if landowners are ever left to grumble when they do nothing to the Creole man they trusted. They don't want to become homeless like some traditional people of West Papua in Thailand. This type of education is creating awareness among the natives of Sierra Leone who just want to live peacefully in their native lands until their natural deaths, and that is what we refer to as "we don't want any problem".

When children enter secondary school, they commence part-2 of the educational foundation years and are mandated to spend five years (Form-1 to Form-5), after which they take the General Certificate of Education (GCE) Ordinary Level. The GCE'O'Level was meant to assess the academic qualifications of school leavers who completed parts 1 and 2 of the education foundation years, ready to pursue further education into post-secondary academic or vocational qualification levels. The University of Sierra Leone required 5 subjects, including

English Language and Mathematics, with no more than two sittings allowed.

Schools in those days immediately after independence in 1961 were very few, and therefore the standard of education was unquestionable, especially during the administration of Sir Milton Margai and Sir Albert Margai, the first two Prime Ministers from the same political party, The Sierra Leone Peoples Party (SLPP), which ruled after independence.

Primary School Teachers with Sixth-Form Qualifications:

Sixth Form was the next stage of post-secondary school education. The sixth form qualification of Advanced Level (A'Level) was highly respected, and many students from Sierra Leone were immediately accepted for university studies directly at Durham University in the UK. This stage was completed in preparation for further education studies at the university level at Fourah Bay College, which was affiliated with Durham University in the UK. Those who completed the sixth form after secondary school were more highly advanced in academic knowledge than primary school teachers and were capable of teaching high standards of mathematics such as geometry, algebra, and so on.

They were employed in schools to teach at SP-1 and SP-2. The problem that arose with these teachers was that although they proved to be the best, these sixth form leavers were too focused on going to university, and they became difficult to handle by primary school teachers, especially those who did not attend secondary school. However, the two years of SP-1 and SP-2 were discontinued, and primary school years reverted to eight years. The main reason for discontinuing the SP-1 and SP-2 levels was that the sixth-form graduate qualification holders were attractive to employers and were more interested in pursuing university qualifications to achieve degree standards, which were more respectable. Having such qualifications at that standard, especially when graduates were young, made them more attractive to many higher-paid job opportunities. You see, university graduates in the days of the SLPP under the Margais were provisionally left to choose from high-level employment. We are praying for those days to return in Sierra Leone.

1967–1968: Andrew Juxon-Smith

Andrew Juxon-Smith was a military officer who eventually became a politician in Sierra Leone and briefly head of state between 27 March 1967 and 18 April 1968, serving as Chairman of the National Reformation Council and acting Governor General. Juxon-Smith's military junta did not last long but was eventually overthrown by junior ranks under the direction of John Amadu Bangura in April 1968. He restored parliamentary rule to Sierra Leone under Siaka Stevens, who later executed John Bangura out of fear for his own life and power, because he perceived Bangura as a threat to his leadership.

During his short term, Juxon-Smith proved to be a military disciplinarian and introduced a series of civil service disciplines, which served as a wake-up call for workers to report early for duties. He also introduced street cleaning in Freetown, known as "Keep-the-City Clean," a practice somewhat maintained by subsequent governments. As a follow-up legacy, the current civilian democratic government headed by Julius Maada Bio is maintaining the national cleaning program, which requires everyone to participate in community cleaning on National Cleaning Day.

1967: The Commencement of Political Disunity in Sierra Leone (and its effects on education):

Sierra Leone remained under the leadership of Sir Milton Margai as Prime Minister until Siaka Stevens, a member of the SLPP, broke away and formed a new political party called the All Peoples Congress (APC).

When Siaka Stevens rigged the parliamentary elections in 1977, the APC held 74 seats, and the SLPP had 15. In 1978, the APC forced a new political system called "One Party democracy," which Siaka Stevens pushed parliament to approve. A decree forced all parliament members, including those from the SLPP opposition headed by Salia Jusu Sheriff, to declare support for the one-party state and become members of the APC by force. This was one of the menaces of Siaka Stevens's dictatorial politics, which crushed anything that stood in his way.

1970s: The Beginning of Politics' Harmful Impact on Education in the 1970s:

The 1970s saw the political agenda disinterest in education, partly because the APC administration was in physical confrontation with college students and the Sierra Leone Labour Congress.

This explains why the opposition described the APC party as mostly petty traders, taxi drivers, and thugs associated with violence, showing little interest in the education of the nation's children.

Siaka Stevens was known to rule Sierra Leone with an iron fist through violence in his political campaign for APC recognition. Many Sierra Leoneans were uncomfortable with his rule, as this style of political violence was unexpected in their political leadership.

Another of his disregard was towards education enthusiasts. He did not believe in achievement through education but through fighting to retain political power. He convinced many young people that politics was the only way forward for job advancement, especially in the civil service. Those who openly supported his party were promoted to higher positions and offices without merit, promoted above those who had served longer, to ensure respect for APC supporters. School leavers with few Ordinary level qualifications were rapidly recruited and promoted to Permanent Secretary positions in government ministries and as District Officers (DOs) overseeing district headquarters, ruling over university graduates. Additionally, there was a withholding of educational support from universities down to primary schools. The word scholarship disappeared from his vocabulary, as he claimed education was an individual right and privilege for those who could afford it. The few scholarships he approved for university places were distributed through tribalism based on applicants' areas of origin and surnames, all administered centrally at the Ministry of Education under Permanent Secretary Mr. W.B. Munu, who expected a "fat brown envelope" before checking anyone's application file.

Some of us never went through university doors in our country because we could not afford brown envelopes for the Ministry of Education's permanent secretary.
Another area of corruption Siaka Stevens encouraged was derailing the decentralization of the civil service operating system initiated by the British and left to Sierra Leone, shifting from district headquarters to a centralized system at the Ministry of Education in Freetown. This was intended to streamline control over Sierra Leonean communities not supportive of APC politics. Some of us were not only uninterested in politics but did not even understand or believe in these crooked methods.
Scholarship applicants were identified and scrutinized by their surname and district of origin, which defined who succeeded, not by their educational qualifications.
As Almighty God sees everything under the sun, the Holy Spirit saw my predicament with APC selection methods and directed me to apply for further education in the UK through an advertisement I discovered in the West African magazine. That year, I was the first Sierra Leonean to apply, and within two weeks, I received a letter from the Institute of Commercial Management in Bournemouth, UK. I completed the application form, and within another two weeks, I received an offer for full-time studies for two years, with a full grant.
Siaka Stevens's leadership style earned the nickname "putting the square peg in a round hole," but he was comfortable with this because it gave him total power over government authorities, breeding those in power who were unqualified but had the abilities to intimidate opponents of his political views.

As a school dropout without a certificate, Stevens began a career in the Sierra Leone Police Force as a stray-dogs handler, later abandoning this to work as a mine laborer at the Marampa Iron-Ore Mines in his home district in the Northern Province.

He continued working there and joined the Sierra Leone Labour Congress trade union. Later, he attended a seminar for trade union aspirants at Roskin College in Oxford, UK, which lasted a few days, where he received a certificate of attendance.

On returning to Sierra Leone, he claimed to have completed a trade union diploma course in Oxford and began canvassing for recognition among trade union members, promising rights at work. Eventually, he was made chairman of the Sierra Leone Labour Congress.

Siaka Stevens was uncomfortable with educated people, claiming they could not easily agree with him, even when he thought something was sensible. He said, “It is not books that make sense, but sense makes books.” His mindset seriously undermined the educational benefits of the nation. Valuing money more than educational achievements, he coined the proverb “Where they tie the cow is where it must graze”, which sowed the seed for corruption in the civil service. This seed germinated and engulfed all aspects of the Sierra Leonean workforce, encouraging the offering of “brown envelopes” for official matters.

All educational matters were centrally administered at the Ministry of Education in Freetown, including approval of teachers’ qualifications and payment of their salaries. This centralization still exists today and has been accepted by all governments as the landmark of educational administration

with no attempts at reform. Furthermore, all government ministries are centralized in Freetown, while the lives of Sierra Leoneans evolve in other parts of the country, such as Bo, Kenema, Kailahun, Makeni, Port Loko, Bonthe, Moyamba, and other areas (This is absolutely wrong)!
Schools faced disturbances due to the general transportation system, deeply affecting many schools in Freetown and other major cities. There was a railway transportation system connected to many destinations in the provinces, mainly serving farming communities to transport their products cheaply to markets, especially in the eastern province of Kailahun District. The railway was very useful for transporting farm goods to the ports in Freetown for shipment to overseas markets where they were highly demanded for processing for human consumption.

The railway transportation services were not only for farmers but also facilitated schoolchildren traveling from far-off homes to school on time, especially for morning classes, with cheaper fares. This comfortable and convenient transportation in Freetown and the provinces was abandoned by the APC administration under Siaka Stevens, who preferred road transportation by heavy trucks and lorries without considering the high costs of road maintenance and frequent traffic jams during busy hours.

Since that time, road accidents on busy roads have increased substantially, and many children have become demotivated from schooling due to lack of transportation and have dropped out. However, the SLPP administration of Maada Bio is working to improve transportation for schoolchildren in Freetown. As gradual movements carry the African sparrow birds into dustbins to feed better, we are satisfied with the SLPP under Maada Bio's administration due to positive initiatives still on the agenda, primarily to make education free for all children in government schools in Sierra Leone, even if the parents are not Sierra Leoneans, provided they live, work, and pay taxes in Sierra Leone.

This railway transportation system was one of the assets the British left with Sierra Leone after independence.

Employment of school teachers was managed by school headmasters/mistresses/principals in all schools, including provincial ones. When a school hired a teacher, for example, in a village in the Eastern Province, the teacher remained unpaid until Ministry of Education approval in Freetown was granted and sent back to the school. Under Siaka Stevens's APC administration, this approval was mandatory before the teacher could receive a salary. Was this a fair system to punish teachers by withholding their salaries? If this system still operates, it is absolutely wrong at the national educational institution management level.

Many teachers suffered due to this approval system. Teachers working for six months without salary had to travel to the Ministry of Education in Freetown to chase approval for their pay, which clerks often delayed. The Ministry's location in Freetown posed an additional obstacle as most provincial teachers did not know anyone there or had never been there before; but that was not considered.

Such trips required teachers to borrow money for travel, accommodation, and bribes ("brown envelopes") to clerks. When teachers finally received approval, they often faced significant debt from these expenses. This was a major bottleneck for teachers in Sierra Leone. Landlords in some cities refused to rent houses to teachers because of their salary delays due to Ministry circumstances.

Siaka Stevens knew these hardships but called it a new administrative system to control education.

Gradually, many good teachers, even those with professional qualifications, left teaching for jobs in civil service and private organizations, leaving schools nearly empty of qualified teachers. One must ask: what is the condition of an educational authority without good teachers?

1970: Treason Trial Executions (Methods of removing Siaka Stevens's opponents)

The Head of Sierra Leone Military Forces, Brigadier-General John Amadu Bangura, was accused of conspiracy to stage a political coup and executed on 29 March 1970, sending shockwaves that Stevens would not compromise even with high-ranking opponents.

1972: Change from Common Entrance Examination to Selective Entrance Examination

In 1972, the late Minister of Education J. Bathes Wilson announced changes to the school examination system, replacing the Common Entrance Examination with the Selective Entrance Examination. This reduced the duration of primary education from eight to six years.

This meant the number of hours scheduled for primary education was drastically cut by two years, accompanied by a reduction in syllabus content.

Thus, this period marks when school education standards began to decline, during Siaka Stevens's early APC regime. Though Minister Wilson announced the change, it was clear that President Siaka Stevens approved and directed this.

Late President Siaka Stevens was aware of and endorsed the systematic lowering of education standards in Sierra Leone, even as his children and those of ministers received quality education abroad in the UK and USA, expenses fully covered by the Sierra Leone government. These children were expected to return home to occupy government ministries as "bosses" over less-educated citizens. However, some of these "political boys" ended up involved in drugs and prostitution abroad, dropping out and never returning home, eventually living in ghettos in US cities.

1973: The Selective Entrance Examination (SEE)

The Common Entrance Examination was replaced in 1973 but remained under the control of the West African Examinations Council (WAEC), in existence since 1952. By then, the education system in Sierra Leone was under government control since independence in 1961, with the British colonial system having left.

Schoolchildren then experienced the importance of passing external examinations. The history somewhat repeated itself from the Church Missionary Society (CMS) system of education in the 1780s, which locals once criticized as "very bookish," particularly for non-Christian Sierra Leonean children.

Two years were taken off the stipulated eight years for primary education, reducing it to six, despite educational sustainability demanding eight years minimum. The APC

government under Late President Siaka Stevens did not consider the spill-over effects of these government decisions, which left substantial gaps in the education system that are difficult to rectify.

Primary school was now scheduled from class one to class six, without nursery schools except in some private institutions in larger cities for rich students. The importance of nursery school (under five) education is crucial as the friendships children establish early remain lifelong, and one major benefit of education is to enable individuals to select their lifelong friends.

1974: Another Treason Trial Execution:

Siaka Stevens continued accusing high-ranking personalities in the country falsely of plotting political coups against his government and had his opponents executed, including those in 1974.

Siaka Stevens years of reign in Sierra Leone left a freight of terror about politics in the minds of most of us who grew up in Sierra Leone in the 1970s- at the time of his reign, which left us with no alternative but to wash our hands off from developing interests in politics even when the talents exist.

Politics was a life gambling game in Sierra Leone (To die or to leave) and that is why some of us up to this day, don't even think of getting closer to politics, because the game of politics is just very dirty and tasteless.

We only depend on educational achievements as genuine life success wherever we may find ourselves in the world. Education can take you anywhere around the globe but Sierra Leone politics takes you to frustration and deaths before your natural death and go to hell to continue suffering in eternity. I don't want to end that way; do you?

Politicians are the saddest and the most disillusioned in most societies, especially My best advice to all school children is to concentrate and work harder in your educational pursuits and don't envy politicians and go with the feelings that they are really enjoying.

ours in Sierra Leone. Most of them are fakes and you are even in better conditions because you go to bed and sleep well till next morning when your parents wake you up to get ready and go to school; but politicians have no rest and some of them are even afraid of sleeping at home, in their houses they are squandering money from the state to build.

What I do not personally agree with politicians with, in the African Politics and African Politicians Behaviour is when they are continuously engaged into spending the small amount of money in our African countries into buying arms and ammunitions of guns and bombs to kill those who do not agree with them and their policies in the country they rule. This is nor fair because those who don't agree with them are still their own brothers and sisters (nationals) in the country and in this 21st century. Must we now not take on-board that we are practising democratic politics where we don't always agree with each other? Therefore, we agree to disagree. Where this is the fact, why the grumbling and uneasiness of our politicians, resulting into rebel wars of civil conflicts that is unsettling Africa?

1976: Another Treason Trial Execution Again:

Brigadier David Lansana,
Mohamed Sorie Forna,
Journalist/Politician Ibrahim Bash Taqi, and
Lieutenant Habib Lansana Kamara.

The All Peoples Congress (APC) government in Sierra Leone was known for deliberate killings and destruction of human lives—killing seasons of my country. In 1976, these high-caliber military personnel, among many others, were all removed from Siaka Stevens's path through execution. (This part of the writing reflects incidents I witnessed in Sierra Leone as a secondary school student at Methodist Boys' High School in Freetown in the 1970s; no additional reference is required to explain this).

Siaka Stevens capitalized on the religious instincts of many Sierra Leoneans to continue violating human rights against anyone who stood in his political way, which made him the "Adolf Hitler" of West Africa, turning Sierra Leone into a living hell where all ambitions of determined young Sierra Leoneans were crushed. Politics thus became a dirty game designed to crush young lives at the slightest mistake.

Special teacher training arrangements, if not already included in the teacher training curriculum in Sierra Leone, should be developed specifically for teachers dealing with early-year learners at the start of schooling.

In 1973, the Selective Entrance Examination (SEE) was introduced for primary schools, and this examination is, to this date, still conducted by the West African Examinations Council (WAEC).

The former Common Entrance Examination (CEE) focused on Arithmetic Calculations and English Communication skills, but this was watered down by the introduction of the Selective

Entrance Examination, which shifted to more multiple-choice questions encouraging guesswork. This examination does not indicate whether candidates pass or fail but produces total grade scores according to the child's capabilities. Secondary schools admitted students based on their SEE scores at their discretion. Since all schools charged fees on admission, most admitted students who were financially able to pay tuition.

This system encouraged a high level of corruption because wealthy parents could send their children to prestigious schools without the normal passing grades, so long as they could afford the fees.

This educational foundation calamity in Sierra Leone parallels the "The Death and Life of the Great American School System" as exposed by Diane Ravitch (2010).

Since 1973, there has been a "water-down" effect on primary school education and examination standards, which has expanded to secondary education, resembling a "garbage-in, garbage-out" system.

However, a vast difference exists in today's SEE compared with the Common Entrance Examination, which still contains uncountable loopholes causing drops in primary education standards. These drops continue to affect both primary and post-secondary standards. Research has begun revisiting the history of education in Sierra Leone and possibly across Anglophone West African countries, including Ghana, Nigeria, The Gambia, and Liberia (under American influence), all under the examination supervision of the West African Examinations Council (WAEC) since 1952.

WAEC is an examining body, distinct from the Ministry of Education, Science, and Technology of Sierra Leone. Research evidence has not yet produced a new national education curriculum and review reports required by the Ministry to be taught in all schools. This means Sierra Leone's educational standards are far below global standards. Constant changes occur worldwide, but Sierra Leone's standards lag and struggle to adapt. Although the new SLPP government under President Maada Bio makes desperate efforts to standardize the system, success has not yet materialized on the global education stage for our hungry children. The system's foundation was left neglected too long, making it difficult to provide adequate education for our children's needs.

One WAEC responsibility is to provide external examinations yearly for schools, but are they constantly receiving curriculum reviews? When I contacted the Ministry of Education in Freetown in 1997 during the APC regime to view such documents, they were unavailable.

Since its foundation, politics have seriously infiltrated WAEC operations negatively, devaluing its credibility with employers and post-secondary institutions. The public, left with no alternative, has had to rely on its services as the only option. "Take what you have in your possession, until you get what you want," says a Creole parable. As the APC political system cannot provide tangible evidence of educational support, the education system has been in danger for a long time. Immediate rectification is necessary, especially for primary and secondary education.

This should not be left to politicians, who have the financial means to send their children abroad to good schools but leave most good talents wasted because their parents cannot afford overseas education. The government under Siaka Stevens never assisted children without APC connections, especially from eastern and southern provinces. These children are my concern and focus because I believe they possess quality human resources vital for Sierra Leone. Some APC-sponsored children became stuck in America, dropping out and living in New York ghettos unfit for humans.

1977: Nationwide Student Demonstrations against the APC Government of Siaka Stevens:

Siaka Stevens's APC rule was seriously challenged by massive national student demonstrations in 1977, led by Student Union President Hindolo Trye at Fourah Bay College, which highlighted government mismanagement and neglect of learning facilities in all educational sectors.

1985: New President through Change of APC Leadership (Conspiracy against Vice President Mr. Sorie Ibrahim Koroma):

Stevens ensured security by appointing a leader for the APC who would not be questioned. He appointed Military Commander Brigadier Joseph Saidu Momoh as head of state in 1985.

In 1985, Major-General Joseph Momoh succeeded Stevens as president. By the late 1980s, economic conditions worsened, and there was growing demand for constitutional reform. The government set up a constitutional review commission.

The commission's recommendation of a return to multiparty democracy was overwhelmingly endorsed in a referendum in August 1991. During Momoh's APC administration, education services deteriorated; many schools lacked basic learning facilities like desks and chairs and received no government support. Teacher salaries were delayed or unpaid, and auxiliary staff such as cleaners were paid by schools themselves. This marked the start of desperate times for schools, as few trained, willing teachers lacked facilities, materials, and motivation to teach and encourage students. What was the world moving toward?

1991–2002: THE SIERRA LEONE CIVIL WAR YEARS:

In 1991, civil war broke out in Sierra Leone, spilling over from neighboring Liberia. The Revolutionary United Front (RUF), starting in March 1991, later became a political party negotiated into the post-war government under Sierra Leone Peoples Party (SLPP) leader President Ahmad Tejan Kabbah.

The RUF was led by a Sierra Leonean from Tonkolili district discovered to be a relative of former President Siaka Stevens. Foday Sankoh was recruited into the Sierra Leone Military Forces by Stevens as an APC supporting agent. During the 1976 executions of high-caliber military personnel, including cabinet minister Mohamed Sorie Forna, Sankoh was listed among coup plotters against Stevens.

At his coup trial, Sankoh was charged with 'mis-treason of treason'; his punishment was commuted from execution to life imprisonment in Pademba Road Prison, Freetown.

While serving his sentence and after the executions, Stevens summoned Sankoh, reprimanded him, and finally pardoned him according to the constitution, warning him not to return to Tonkolili District, which Sankoh accepted.

Upon release, Sankoh settled near Segbwema in the Eastern Province near Liberia, where he started a photography business operating among Mende-Kissy tribes close to the Liberian border. His location was strategic, allowing easy border crossings without immigration checks, enabling involvement in illegal diamond mining and arms importation through Liberia. Sankoh's friend Charles Taylor introduced him to contacts interested in trading war rifles in exchange for Sierra Leone diamonds, rapidly procuring "Kalashnikov AK-47" rifles from Ukraine suppliers to fuel the conflict of fratricidal violence.

1992: Military Takeover:

On 29 April 1992, junior military officers led by young Valentine Strasser staged a coup over President Joseph Saidu Momoh. Soldiers arrived at State House in Freetown requesting supplies urgently needed at the war front. The president was absent, and his secretary informed him. Alarmed, Momoh fled by helicopter into exile in Guinea-Conakry, leaving the country to the soldiers who overthrew his APC government. Strasser, nearing his 25th birthday with a sixth-form qualification, was chosen leader and became Sierra Leone's youngest president.

1996: Palace Coup on Valentine Strasser:

On 29 April 1992, Bio was among young soldiers including Captain Valentine Strasser, lieutenants Sahr Sandy, Solomon Musa, Tom Nyuma, and Captain Komba Mondeh who toppled Momoh's APC government in a bloodless coup, forming the National Provisional Ruling Council (NPRC) with Strasser as leader.

On 16 January 1996, Julius Maada Bio, Strasser's deputy, staged a coup, ousting Strasser into exile in Guinea-Conakry—the palace coup of Sierra Leone, as it was staged by the head of state's deputy. Notably, Bio did not kill Strasser despite opportunity; instead, he sent him into exile for his safety.

Strasser remains alive in Sierra Leone under President Julius Maada Bio's care and protection. Observing human rights and dignity, Strasser is alive though unemployed. He may become another head of state; only God decides. Killing has never been on Bio's agenda, and we pray for divine sustenance on this hope.

1996: Democratic Transition:

The NPRC under Brigadier General Julius Maada Bio organized transfer to civilian politicians. Ahmed Tejan Kabbah won SLPP leadership and the 1996 multiparty elections, becoming known as Sierra Leone's wartime president.

However, he was deposed for over a year by a military coup led by Johnny Paul Koroma, released from prison to undermine Kabbah. Many believed the opposition APC orchestrated this. Koroma had formed the Armed Forces Revolutionary Council (AFRC). Kabbah ruled in exile in Guinea until restored by ECOWAS military forces in 1998.

Kabbah, a former UN civil servant valuing education, led restoration efforts for damaged schools countrywide. He pledged on election eve to end civil war and bring peace—and he delivered, demonstrating skill and patience unknowable to rebel leader Sankoh.

School survival was impossible in many areas during war; fears of children being abducted as child soldiers halted schooling and assessments.

1998: ECOMOG Restores Kabbah:

Kabbah was elected in 1996 amid civil war but briefly ousted by APC coup in 1997, forcing exile. ECOWAS forces restored him in 1998.

He opened peace talks with rebel leader Sankoh to end conflict and established peace. Kabbah's UN diplomatic experience lent him strong loyalty to Sierra Leone's peace.

He granted rebels amnesty and appointed Sankoh vice president responsible for minerals including diamonds. Though some question this decision, Sankoh was given secure residence and office, but the arrangement alienated him from rebel supporters, leading to loss of control and frustration—history records the aftermath.

Kabbah prioritized renovating village schools while in exile, normalizing education delivery. He waived examination fees for eligible pupils taking the West African Secondary School Certificate Examination (WASSCE), beneficial especially to families with multiple children.

Kabbah ended a decade-long civil war and restored peace by 2002; he died on 13 March 2014. He is remembered as Sierra Leone's wartime president who spent much of his tenure negotiating peace. He promised and he delivered.

2017: Discovery of Part of My Education Research Visit Earlier in 2017

My previous research on education centered on provinces in the North, East, and South of Sierra Leone, covering:

- Bo district
- Kenema district
- Kailahun district
- Tonkolili district
- Moyamba district
- Bombali district
- Koinadugu district
- Kono district
- Pujehun district
- Bonthe district
- Port Loko district
- Kambia district
- (which existed before the APC regime's later political rearrangements).

The areas of Freetown and Greater Freetown provinces were not covered during my MA (Education) research visit in 2017 because education problems there were far greater—outweighing those in the other twelve districts.

The development of education in Freetown (the capital city) is far greater than that in the twelve districts. This, among other reasons, has created a magnetic clustering effect of the entire population into Freetown, leading to unbearable human living conditions and various environmental and socio-economic problems. Recently, landslides at Sugarloaf Mountain near Freetown resulted in thousands of uncovered bodies caused by population influx seeking dwellings—a typical human existence pattern. Politicians with high wealth seized this opportunity, turning it into an investment haven by building fine dwellings for housing seekers who pay rents directly into these corrupt politicians' bank accounts.

It is important to note that nursery, primary, and secondary education has never been free in Sierra Leone, although the government's ultimate goal has been to provide free primary education. Access has only been possible where parents or guardians were willing and able to pay the required fees, or else children without payment ability were sent home by schools.

"No fees, no education" was the practice then and fertile ground for private education providers and schools which boomed, despite some published sources boasting of free primary education. Such claims were mere political propaganda to "whitewash" political benefits to Sierra Leoneans.

The government and civil society recognize the importance of free universal primary education, yet about half a million children remain out of school—out of approximately 7 million population according to the APC regime's census—with many youths lacking skills, so much work remains.

How the "Two-Seems" Stand in the Constitution of Sierra Leone:

A constitution is primarily a set of rules specifying governance, power distribution, control, and citizens' rights.

It is typically written and contained in a single document. Sierra Leone's constitution is unusual, being uncodified with many sources.

Nonetheless, in 1863, Sierra Leone became the first British colony in West Africa to adopt a constitution—the Blackhall Constitution—named for the then-governor, comprising Legislative and Executive Councils.

Article: Sierra Leone: Constitutional Amendment Passed by Legislature (Nov. 26, 2013)

On November 19, 2013, the House of Representatives (unicameral Parliament) passed a controversial constitutional amendment.

Though the first adopted draft is not included here, records show the first constitution has gone through many changes and amendments up to November 26, 2013, via parliamentary debates.

Since such amendments can fundamentally change a country's political system, they follow prescribed procedures. For example, the Nineteenth Amendment, granting US women the right to vote, was a landmark change recognizing women as citizens and taxpayers.

In the UK, constitutional amendments abolished the death sentence, including for murder, following the case of Ruth Ellis, the last woman hanged on July 13, 1955, by hangman Albert Pierrepoint. She was pardoned because she was deemed not in her right mind at the time of the crime. This "law of social justice" influenced English law and is now adopted in Sierra Leone under the SLPP government led by Julius Maada Bio; well done.

However, I struggle with how these rules apply to those committing failed political coups—seeking power democratically but committing mass civilian murders and warfare. Should they be exempt from capital punishment using "diminishing responsibility," as applied in 2023 under the SLPP government?

Sierra Leone's political constitution has experienced complexity, prompting political actors to be cautious to avoid regret. In 1977, student demonstrations challenged APC rule. In 1978, Siaka Stevens forced "one-party democracy," winning approval despite previous rejection. Members of opposition who failed to join the APC within thirty days forfeited parliamentary seats. SLPP MPs, including leader Salia Jusu Sheriff, joined APC reluctantly to protect constituencies. The last to join was Hon. George Kpeguay Saffa of Kenema district.

A major constitutional clause bars those with dual nationality from political participation. Many Sierra Leoneans reside abroad (UK, US, Europe, Africa), holding dual nationality for better access to jobs and education. This is acceptable if they obey host country laws.

However, it is against human rights for all Sierra Leoneans, home and diaspora, to manipulate the constitution for political gain. Constitutional changes must benefit all registered parties, not just one. Amendments require careful parliamentary consideration.

Sierra Leoneans with dual nationality must be honest. Are they entering politics to access and transfer the country's meager income abroad, enriching themselves while leaving Sierra Leone impoverished? Sierra Leoneans are aware, and the constitution protects all citizens. Genuine national interest must prevail over exploiting politics for personal gain. Such lifestyles are degrading, and corrupt politicians and their foreign-based elites are increasingly exposed and rejected.

Most diaspora Sierra Leoneans (except Creoles) originate from villages needing water, electricity, schools with libraries, toilets, computers, internet, and international-standard education. Supporting constituency needs would be meaningful, but playing politician while abroad is questionable and risky.

Policy Issue:

Elections are major public investments. The UNDP, the largest donor, spent over three billion dollars supporting elections in low-income countries in 15 years (UNDP 2019). Election quality depends on candidate selection.

Most democracies rely on party officials to nominate candidates. Party leaders may be better informed on qualifications but may value party loyalty or ability to pay for nomination, traits unrelated to effective governance. Voters often lack information to choose the best candidates. Limited evidence exists on resolving trade-offs between uninformed voters and officials valuing different candidate traits, as political leaders rarely vary candidate selection. Are voters or party officials better placed to select candidates? Could more democratic primaries involving voter input and reliable qualification information improve elections by electing more representative and competent leaders?

The Up to Date of The Constitutional Change in Sierra Leone.

The death sentence, which is known as the capital punishment is now dropped or abolished and replaced with a period of "Thirty- Years Gail in Prison" in the West African state of Sierra Leone. The last capital punishment took place in 1988 when 23 soldiers were executed through firing for treasonable offences against democratically elected government of Sierra Leone Peoples' Party (SLPP) under the administration of President Ahmad Tejan Kabbah. This amendment took place in July 2021 but in June 2021, "99 people have already been placed on death role sentences to death but not yet executed". What do you think is happening to them?

Context of the Evaluation:

Sierra Leone's Parliament comprises 132 constituencies, each electing one Member of Parliament (MP) to represent approximately 40,000 local residents in the national government. Voting patterns tend to reflect historic relationships between ethnic groups and the two major political parties—the Sierra Leone Peoples' Party (SLPP) and the All People's Congress (APC)—while other political parties have emerged over the years.

Although the APC and SLPP differ in how they select candidates to compete in general elections, both parties share the characteristic that ordinary party members and the broader voting public do not directly participate or formally vote in either party's primary selection process.

Previous research suggests that elected MPs underperform. For example, one study that examined MP spending found that only 36 percent of discretionary public funds controlled by MPs could be verified as spent on development projects in their constituencies. Additionally, MPs on average made only four public statements during more than 50 sittings of Parliament and held only one meeting with their constituents during their first year in office.

Voters, party officials, and potential candidates exhibited different levels of education and wealth. Voters in this study had, on average, completed five years of education; 43 percent had no formal schooling, and only four percent had attended university. Potential candidates, by contrast, had completed over 15 years of education on average, none lacked formal schooling, and 80 percent had university education. Party officials were in between these groups, with 12 years of education on average, five percent without schooling, and 34 percent with some university education. In terms of wealth, voters owned fewer assets and were much less likely to have a formal bank account than party officials or potential aspirants. Elections are male-dominated: 80 percent of party officials and 90 percent of aspirants were male, compared to 47 percent of registered voters.

The constitution of Sierra Leone further specifies qualifications to run for the office of president:

Candidates must be one hundred percent Sierra Leonean, meaning both parents must be nationals of the country.

If both parents are Sierra Leoneans but the child, male or female, is born outside Sierra Leone, such persons are not qualified to hold the presidential position.

Sierra Leoneans holding dual nationality with other countries are not allowed to participate in the country's leadership contests.

All political leaders in Sierra Leone must be literate with the ability to read, write fluently, and communicate well in English—the country's official language and lingua franca—for effective parliamentary debate.

Children born in Sierra Leone to foreign nationals will be disqualified from becoming president if their parents' nationalities were not changed to Sierra Leone nationals before the children's birthdays. If parental nationality changes occurred before the children's birthdays, such children qualify to become president.

Sierra Leoneans who give birth outside the country's boundaries cannot have their children contest for political leadership or presidency in Sierra Leone upon reaching adulthood.

EDUCATION PSYCHOLOGY IN THE WAY WE SPEAK AND PRONOUNCE LANGUGES;

Our first teachers, from whom we begin to learn after birth, are our mothers because they are usually our first contact with the world and are happy with the joy of our birth. They draw us closer, smiling happily, and give us our natural food, milk from their breast, which we suck comfortably on their lap.

As we grow up, we do all the inconvenient, nasty things on her lap without care until we begin to talk—at first without understanding what we are saying, either correctly, inappropriately, or wrongly.

What is involved in this learning process are the behavioral attitudes at home between the parents (father and mother).

Basically, we learn to observe and hear from our parents.

When a child undertakes this learning process after birth and is opened to the environment of both the birthplace (country) steadily, the child will learn to know perfectly well the way human beings speak in that country permanently. The development of this accent grows into a kind of sense of permanent belonging to the environment called an accent. This is a natural identity of a group of people who pronounce words in a similar fashion and can easily understand each other. These methods of pronouncing some words in their way of talking are naturally kept permanently, even if they move from their birth countries or origins.

All over the UK and Ireland (in England, Scotland, Wales, and Ireland), we all communicate in the common language of English, but with different accents in different locations. Sometimes it is even difficult to understand when some people talk fast in their dialects. I personally gained experience when my university studies took me around the country to London, Bournemouth, Sunderland, Dundee, Hertfordshire, and Portsmouth in search of different qualifications with a keen eagerness to learn and to teach others.

WHAT WE MUST LEARN NOW FROM THIS EXPERIENCE IN SIERRA LEONE:

There is a high-fly-out political gimmick going around in our country Sierra Leone, and I am just trying to, like any other civilized educated Sierra Leonean, relate to the underlying theories explained above, which I explain as follows:

Our president, Julious Maada Bio, met his present wife, now our First Lady Mrs. Fatima Bio, in the country at a birthday party in South London after a painful divorce from his previous wife in America. At that time, Maada was pursuing his presidential position and heavily campaigning to develop the SLPP membership supporters and donors in the UK.

According to Lady Fatima herself, she went directly to Maada Bio and asked him for a dance. When Maada responded favorably and stood up to dance, she pinched his bottom while pressing on his chest and licking his ears gently like a snake. Then Maada Bio started breathing faster and whispered the words into his ear, “Are you alright?” “Oh yes, I am alright.” As they proceeded with the dance, Fatima raised her head from Maada's shoulder and looked into his eyes and said, "Honey, I want you to marry me because my heart has told me that you are the only man of my life. I am interested in your career in politics; and me becoming your wife will yield added advantage to make you win and become famous as the best president Sierra Leone has ever had, hence I am also in the film acting business at the Nollywood studio in Nigeria."

That was how their love connection started in Southwark, South London. They had their first Muslim wedding in 2013 to satisfy Fatima's Islamic faith. However, on 21 February 2020, President Bio finally took his Christian vow with his wife in the Roman Catholic Church, with Lady Fatima recognized as the First Lady of Sierra Leone. By then, President Bio was already in the third year of the first phase of his term of office as president of the country. There was high skepticism about this marriage in the eyes of many well-wishers, especially when the SLPP was still in its prime under the leadership of Julius Maada Bio; but Fatima had total control over her husband, as is common in most marriages. She forced her way, even threatening Maada Bio's life with words like, "Maada Bio must marry me now! Do you know when Maada Bio is going to die?" which was widely spread on social media.

As the couple first met in London, Fatima later moved to Freetown with his children, leaving the Southwark council flat empty, while many other homeless Londoners were still waiting in the queue for houses, and opposition supporters in London raised big alarms in social media footage.

Life on the ground in Freetown has so far been romantic, especially on the political front, and joyous for both Maada and Fatima, particularly in political management. The First Lady has proved to be very supportive of her husband's publicity in managing the Sierra Leone government and has proved to be a good wife—but to what extent? This is what we want to find out further.

THE PROBLEMS OF THE FIRST LADY OF SIERRA LEONE:

The First Lady of Sierra Leone, Mrs. Fatima Jabie-Bio, has proved to be very active and supportive of SLPP politics and activities throughout the country in keeping the flames of the party burning under the administration of President Julius Maada Bio.

Fatima brought in new ideas of operation which no government had ever thought of in the country, especially the political move towards girls' education. She discouraged some parents/guardians from making school girls abandon education to marry men who intended to marry such girls. She ensured that parliament passed a law charging those guilty of such acts with criminal offenses punishable in courts and issuing fines.

Fatima also introduced the 'hands-off our girls' campaign to stop teenage pregnancies, which were very high among teenage schoolgirls who were often pushed into illegal sexual relationships. This was mainly to stop holidaymakers from flaunting money on local girls in parties and nightclubs. Normally, in Sierra Leone, if a teenage girl became pregnant, she abandoned schooling, often not returning due to personal inconveniences. Now, when a teenage girl gets pregnant, she is forced to attend school to continue her education until she takes examinations to justify her qualifications, which could be difficult. This discipline has encouraged many schoolgirls to wait for the appropriate time to marry after completing education. Encouraged by their parents and the SLPP government's provisions to get education foundations, many girls are seriously competing with boys for university places under President Julious Maada Bio's leadership.

Fatima's ideas to encourage schoolgirls' concentration on schooling were robust, and her charitable organizations provided sanitary pads for girls during their monthly periods. As girls were supplied free of charge in schools, this created very high attendance among girls who previously often stayed home during their periods.

Fatima has been vocal about Africa's economy, not only regarding Sierra Leone's SLPP government. She disclosed her hidden agenda during an interview at Harvard University in America, which reached wide social media coverage.

This First Lady, now showing her mindset, has not engaged in SLPP politics as expected but has been involved in an underground political game within SLPP during a period when the party was vulnerable.

Grassroots voters, especially in villages, have discovered the political strategies Fatima has played since the SLPP came to power under President Julious Maada Bio's administration since 4 April 2018:

Fatima has admitted to everyone that she has been playing political games to make herself popular, claiming to be the best female politician in the country with more political skills than others interested in the field.

Fatima has misbehaved and disturbed sectional community political elections of SLPP members in other regions by supporting candidates of her choice, such as in recent women's elections in Kenema and Kailahun—strong SLPP bases—where winners are always the people's choice, not the First Lady's.

Fatima mediated between workers in a diamond mining company owned by South African investors in Kono District, resulting in company closure after a vendetta when she was not recognized as the company's negotiator. Workers lost jobs and income.

Fatima exhibited poor upbringing by Sierra Leone standards, joking in a school devotion about her husband cleaning her during periods, which is inappropriate and contrary to school discipline.

Fatima disrespected cabinet members, calling the First Minister, a Harvard PhD graduate, a "Dog" during frustration about the Kono mining saga despite his successful tenure as Minister of Education.

Fatima disobeyed and confronted the National Women's Election in Kenema, setting rude rules contrary to the returning officer's moderation efforts to restrict mobile phone use in polling booths, which is necessary to prevent election malpractice.

At the last SLPP election chairmanship event at Bintumani Hotel in Freetown, Fatima embarrassed herself by supporting a candidate against the supporters' choice, leading to public provocation and shameful singing targeting her—an embarrassment likely unseen in her life. There was no control over the situation, even though provocation emerged from opposition members. Sensible people avoid such unnecessary trouble.

Fatima has effectively hijacked government administration into family property under her control, acting beyond dictatorship. Sierra Leone has only one president—Julious Maada Bio. His wife was never elected president or head of state.

Fatima acts to gain popularity among natives to become SLPP's flag bearer and eventually president, despite no government role. The respect for the president has become a burden.

Fatima and Maada met in London, UK, and married in a mosque in 2013.

Fatima can only call herself Sierra Leonean by marriage to a Sierra Leone national.

Fatima's father was a Gambian national given permission to mine diamonds in Kono district. He was not a diplomat, contrary to Fatima's claim in media.

Fatima holds dual nationality of the UK and The Gambia, her birth country per her passport.

This clearly means she is not Sierra Leonean.

Fatima has never naturalized her Sierra Leonean citizenship, even politically.

Fatima Jabbie was born in The Gambia to Umar Jabbie, a Gambian national, and Tigidankay, a Sierra Leonean, believed to be a Kono woman from the Eastern province.

Fatima spent five years in The Gambia growing up, adopting the dialect and sense of belonging as a Gambian, which she still speaks and identifies with, a psychological trait that cannot be denied.

These facts about Fatima Jabie Bio mean she does not qualify to contest for SLPP flag bearer or become president of Sierra Leone. Her ambition to be SLPP's flag bearer for the 2028 general election disrespects the constitution. As a Sierra Leonean, Mrs. Fatima Jabie-Bio is strictly advised to refrain from this calamitous dream. She should understand Sierra Leone's politics is no joke. We owe her respect as the president's wife but not political concession. She must understand this if she has her senses intact. We protect Sierra Leone politics carefully, even regarding marriage to nationals and members.

Their marriage has almost become skeptical, and why?

When people decide to get married, the final decision to do so comes from one of them first, with due consideration until it is finally confirmed by both of them. There are a series of considerations to make this possible based on religion, education level, sources of income, tribal understanding, parental approval, future development decisions, and preparation.

The marriage between our President Julious Maada Bio and Fatima Jabie first took place in a London mosque, purposely to satisfy the love he developed for Fatima, a devout Muslim, although Maada Bio is a Roman Catholic Christian by faith. Thereafter, he took his wife Fatima before the Roman Catholic altar in Freetown in the second year of his presidential term.

Was this marriage actually:

a. out of genuine love?

b. was it out of a desire to become famous as the First Lady of Sierra Leone?

c. was it because of grabbing a hold of Sierra Leone politics so that she could secure the presidency and his household properties?

Most Sierra Leoneans have come to realize now that the actual purpose of Lady Fatima proposing marriage to Maada Bio at their first meeting in South London was because Maada Bio was fundraising in London to support his coming presidential election. He was very frustrated with a bitter divorce case with his former wife in America. This was an added advantage to Fatima's proposal, and she wasted no time convincing Maada to take her to the mosque for the wedding ceremony.

Mrs. Fatima Jabbie Bio's recent revelations on social media show that she has long had an interest in politics and has always wanted to become a politician. This First Lady of Sierra Leone has enjoyed high respect and privileges among the people of Sierra Leone, including members of parliament and President Julious Maada Bio's cabinet members, simply because she is the president's wife.

She has been doing and acting in any way she feels like, whether in the wrong or inappropriate manner or not. An example is the public interview she gave at Harvard University just to popularize herself as a politician's wife. She is now focused on traveling to different countries, representing the Sierra Leone government, just to claim the money the government pays ministers for attending meetings and conferences. So the actual ministers end up with nothing to do in the country—the very purpose for which they are appointed. Is this fair treatment of our ministers?

What about the appointment of qualified personnel in the civil service sector?

The First Lady has been handling this and officially approving these personnel on the agreement that a quota of the earned salary for the job be paid into her charities, which are never audited. People are grumbling about her fussiness in commanding the government, while her husband keeps quiet and does nothing to stop her. She has definitely gone beyond her limit, especially since she is not even an appointed member of parliament.

First Lady Fatima Jabbie Bio should first find out how to become a politician in the right way in our country.

Winning the hearts of voters (particularly grassroots voters in the villages) to see you as someone who will help them, not exploit them, is the first thing they should buy from you—not by giving schoolgirls disposable pads and getting them used to using them. Before the SLPP was formed in Sierra Leone and before the formation of political parties, girls and women looked after themselves very decently before disposable pads arrived. So the females of yesterday were more decent than those of today. The next violation of human rights against our president Julious Maada Bio is that our First Lady has, on a few occasions, alleged that it is her husband who takes off her pants and cleans between her legs because she is unable to get up from bed. Of course, that happens between some couples as lovemaking gestures, but that should not be brought to schoolchildren's devotion as a joke to make them laugh. That is disrespect in the highest degree, and we have the right to be very annoyed for our president.

Fatima Bio does all these as kind and invested gestures to make her easily approachable as a kind and funny woman. Bad mannerism in a girl's upbringing, as advised in Proverbs 22:6 in the Holy Bible, is not mentioned in her vocabulary and we are getting fed up with her acquaintances.

Our politics in Sierra Leone is wrapped with careful respect for human dignity, whether an individual is rich or poor. Of course, there are poor people, but they are not really beggars. Those who beg in the street, from door to door to feed themselves, are mostly from far away—in other countries or provinces far from their homes—and have no relatives or anyone to support them. Nobody has the right to treat such beggars badly.

When I was placed on an education project in The Gambia between 1997 and 2003, it was during the height of the rebel war that brought many Sierra Leoneans running to The Gambia for safety. The then-President Yahyya Jammeh opened his country as a refugee safe haven. Most Sierra Leoneans who arrived were trained and qualified school teachers and university lecturers. They occupied teaching jobs in almost all learning institutions there. That year, the WAEC examination results for The Gambia rose to a higher number of passes than expected.

One night, there was an incident of bad behaviour involving breaking into the safes of Gamtel Ltd. telephone lockers and stealing all the money. The company's director then, Mr. Bokarie Njie, remarked, "The police are now looking into the matter, and when the culprits are caught, they will be dealt with seriously because we do not tolerate foreigners running away as refugees coming to our country to destroy our facilities they have come to and been catered for."

After this remark on Gambian television, the thieves were caught—about four of them, all Gambians, all men. We did not hear from Mr. Bokarie Njie again, who earlier represented Gamtel Ltd. on television, nor did we receive his apology to refugees in The Gambia for his earlier remarks.

Although I was not one of the refugees, I counted myself among them, especially since most of my teachers and schoolmates were there. All nationals holding different passports were charged D500 (five hundred Dalasis) per year for residing in The Gambia, whether as refugees from Sierra Leone or from the North Pole.

When former President David Dauda Jawara was invited as an international dignitary by the late Queen Elizabeth II to grace the wedding of Prince Charles and Diana in London, it coincided with an unexpected failed coup planned by Jawara's relative Samba Sayan Kukoi.

Jawara called on Abdou Diouf of Senegal for immediate help. Diouf wasted no time, sending soldiers by helicopter from Senegal immediately to The Gambia. These Senegalese soldiers overwhelmed Kukoi's fighters, leaving them no chance on Gambian soil.

Samba Sayan Kukoi fled for his life through byways to Guinea-Bissau and never returned to The Gambia. Jawara returned to rule The Gambia until 22 July 1994, when 29-year-old soldier Yahyya Jammeh, who was serving at President Jawara's palace, staged a coup that successfully ousted Sir David Dauda Jawara.

Since that failed coup, peace has endured in The Gambia, and we pray to Almighty Jesus that such political turmoil never returns. That failed coup was essential for The Gambia's people; they realized the power and military skills of the Senegalese army. This prompted the two countries to merge, adopting the name "SENEGAMBIA," meaning being in The Gambia equates to being in Senegal in case of trouble, and vice versa. However, the two countries remain distinct; Senegal is French-speaking (Francophone) and The Gambia is English-speaking (Anglophone), per their colonial histories.

However, the Senegambia confederation did not last long due to economic management issues, social relations, religious beliefs, immigration and border control problems, living standards, and other conflicts. Thus, Gambians remained Gambians, Senegalese remained Senegalese, and both respected each country's national territories legally.

Although The Gambia is a narrow strip surrounded almost entirely by Senegal, it has gone through political and educational changes influenced by different political administrations over time. When Jawara was president, primary and secondary educational facilities for foundational learning were very limited and disproportionately offered to certain tribes. Due to political denial and acceptance of this unevenness, many tribes were left out and did not attend school. The main income source is now domestic house cleaning for those streamed to good education in their own countries. Jawara's regime might have left The Gambia far behind had Yahyya Jammeh's coup not come as a surprise.

Yahya Jammeh was pious, with good intentions to develop The Gambia's education to a world stage. He established the University of The Gambia linked with Canada's University of St. Mary's in Halifax. He contacted UK educational consultants, including the Institute of Commercial Management (ICM) based in Bournemouth, which responded favorably about introducing professional commercial education in The Gambia. The packages were meant to benefit secondary schools, further education colleges, and workers in banks, insurance brokers, and civil service.

At the time Jammeh's application arrived at ICM headquarters in 1997, I was working there and preparing to return to Sierra Leone to revamp the ICM program which I started in 1982 at Methodist Boys' High School, Kissy Mess Mess. Civil war in Sierra Leone started in 1991 and was ongoing, with newly elected President Kabbah deposed by Johnny Paul Koroma's coup. The Director of ICM Education called me, saying I was the only staff member capable of delivering the program; that's how I got the Educational Consultancy Job in The Gambia.

I discussed this with my wife and she agreed to wait for me to return after one year. The workload exceeded expectations; the job scheduled for one year lasted five years until I returned to the UK in 2003. While in The Gambia, to assist Sierra Leonean refugees numbering in the thousands, I became Chairman of the Sierra Leone Nationals Union (SLENU), representing them in government matters involving refugees.

I learned that many Gambians married Sierra Leoneans when already married to Gambian women, unknown to the Sierra Leoneans, as it is permitted under Muslim law to do so. The Sierra Leonean women become "unpaid housemaids" responsible for cooking, cleaning, and childcare of their husbands' children. The Gambian wives keep busy watching Nollywood videos.

This behavior is naked slavery in broad daylight against Sierra Leonean women, experienced within marriages in The Gambia. Sierra Leonean women have human rights to marry any nationality, including Gambians they love—but must think twice before accepting, to avoid future calamities evident in Gambian-Sierra Leonean relationships.

A Sierra Leonean teacher in a Roman Catholic school in Serrekunda married a young Gambian secondary school dropout and had two children. He effectively tutored her at home until she passed RSA Stage-1 in bookkeeping. The young woman, once selling peanuts in the school compound, eventually became school bursar and later earned sponsorship to study Stage-2 qualifications in London. He left their boys with his Sierra Leonean father. The boys attended morning schools.

The father could not leave his full-time teaching job from 9:00-5:00 pm to collect the children, so he asked his wife's brother living nearby to collect the boys daily. The uncle agreed on condition of 5 dalasis taxi fare to avoid walking home under the hot afternoon sun. The teacher added 3 dalasis for snacks until he returned home. The wife's brother only collected money but did not put the children in taxis. The young man, unemployed and seeking work, used the money for daily expenses.

One early school closing day, the teacher waited in the veranda worried as the boys hadn't come. After an hour, he saw his boys coming with their uncle, sweating under the hot, dusty streets. The teacher asked, "My friend, why didn't you take a taxi with the children?" The uncle became violent, beating the teacher hard with a stick on the chest, ordering him to keep quiet and never ask again. The teacher's chest organs were damaged; he vomited blood. They tried to take him to Victoria Hospital, but he died en route.

As SLENU Chairman, I contacted Sierra Leone High Commissioner H.E. Morike Fofanah for intervention, since the victim was a Sierra Leonean teacher in The Gambia. Police kept the body in the mortuary until his wife returned from the UK after two weeks.

The investigation concluded it was a family quarrel-turned-accident. The case was handled within the family. The deceased left two children and a surviving wife who must now provide for them. That was another Gambian experience I added to my own, which I continue to share with fellow Sierra Leoneans. I have yet to tell my Gambian story to President Julious Maada Bio; I hope this book serves as my mouthpiece.

One experience learned from The Gambia is the required RESIDENTIAL PERMIT fee of D500.00 paid yearly by all nationals living there with different passports who have lived for three months or more. I believe this fee is for safety protection and goes to national revenue.

I have never heard of Gambians or other nationals paying residential permits in Sierra Leone. I have never heard of foreigners paying such permits here. Are we so rich that we do not need this kind of inland revenue method?

Let us wake up and learn from the experience of economic management in other countries. Economic management should not be confined to the classroom alone to understand demand and supply. As we are now providing FREE QUALITY EDUCATION in all government schools, one of the major sources of obtaining funds for providing "this basic education foundation" for our children growing up in the country is the RESIDENTIAL PERMIT payment of Le500.00 by all foreign nationals living in Sierra Leone. Therefore, if they stay continuously for more than three months, they are eligible to pay the Le500.00 residential permit. Foreign nationals who do not pay this should be arrested and detained in police cells until flights are ready to deport them to their countries of origin according to their passport travel documents, with the flight cost charged to their respective governments.

Political management should not only be left to the "members of your cabinet and members of parliament alone." Civilians like me, who are not politicians but earn a living in different professions, such as teaching, should have a say on economic development matters in our country—

Sierra Leone—although living in the diaspora but a member of SLPP-UK/I. Let us remember that we are not very rich in Sierra Leone, and we have to let foreigners living here understand this. Let us be very honest about our position and not play any generosity because things are getting hard on our pockets.

Social media revelations from different sources suggest that foreign nationals from various African countries should be allowed to live in Sierra Leone with no visas at all. If we are to accept this kind of political change, let us first study the political consequences on those countries that might have already adopted this idea. Do not entertain such suggestions without state approval through a national referendum, especially since the First Lady has already jumped ahead via her social media platform without such agreement, claiming that Gambians are now allowed to live freely in Sierra Leone and Sierra Leoneans are allowed to live freely in The Gambia, as she supposedly negotiated between the two countries.

As the First Lady is your wife now, my advice to you—for your wife—is that her publicity on this sensitive issue without a national referendum has polarized our country, Sierra Leone, and is not going down well with Sierra Leone nationals. I hope she refrains from repeating such publicity mentioning Sierra Leone with the Green, White, and Blue flag.

You must also let her understand that it was not the First Lady of Sierra Leone, Fatima Jabbie-Bio, who elected you to become president of our country. We are aware that she helped you greatly in the presidential campaigns, but she has no right to hold your presidential office. You did not become president through her; she became our First Lady only when you married her in Sierra Leone, and her position remains intact until President Bio leaves office. When Sierra Leone gets another president, not by death but through the usual democratic presidential election in 2028, her status changes to former First Lady, and we will then have a new First Lady with a different identity.

MY BRIEF AUTOBIOGRAPHY:

My name is Mohamed Sannoh, and I have been a school teacher for more than thirty years, starting at the Methodist Boys' High School, Kissy Mess Mess, where I attended all of my secondary education in Freetown and later worked with Mr. Willie O. Pratt when he was the principal. After finishing Form 5, I did not attend Fourah Bay College because I was not awarded a national scholarship by the then APC administration of Siaka Stevens, as I was identified by my surname as the son of parents from Kenema who were SLPP supporters. The permanent secretary chairing my scholarship interview at the Ministry of Education was Mr. W.B. Munu, and I was turned down. My application was therefore unsuccessful, and my personal battle to pursue academic education beyond secondary school and obtain a degree began.

While in secondary school, I embarked on correspondence studies with colleges in Britain offering long-distance courses and eventually earned Diplomas in Successful Salesmanship and in Sales Management and Marketing from Jersey Island in Britain; these were above A-Level qualifications. Curiously reading newspapers, I saw an advertisement in West Africa magazine inviting applications to study at the Business Studies Centre in Bournemouth, England, UK. I immediately rushed to the post office, bought a postal order, wrote and posted my application the same day.

Two weeks later, I received by post the official application form from the Institute of Commercial Management,

Bournemouth. I completed and posted the form the same day along with copies of my diplomas and school leaving certificate, then waited for a reply. My full grant award to study for two years in the UK came by post.

Upon arrival, I was the only Sierra Leonean at the college; other Africans were from Nigeria, Ghana, and others from Singapore, China, and Malaysia. I completed the ICM course and award within six months, having received many exemptions. The Institute was considering establishing training centers worldwide, including in English-speaking countries like Sierra Leone. I proved suitable with the ability and skills to enroll and manage external examinations in Sierra Leone. That is how I got the job as ICM National Representative and was encouraged by Mr. Willie O. Pratt to obtain the ICM course, headquartered at Methodist Boys' High School (MBHS). Another opportunity came when I was seconded to launch the ICM education project in The Gambia after completing my BEd (Hons) Business Education/BA in Commerce and MBA after 10 years in the UK.

I succeeded with flying colours coinciding with educational development under President Yahyya Jammeh. From 1997 to 2002 in The Gambia, I established ICM courses at the Management Development Institute, Gambia Technical Training Institute (GTTI), Nusrat Senior Secondary School (NSSS), and The Institute of Professional Administration and Management (IPAM Gambia) to serve secondary schools, further education colleges for full-time classes, and workers in late afternoon classes.

About 500 young Sierra Leoneans who studied under my invigilation and passed the ICM Certificate in Commercial Studies through my education projects there and at West African Methodist (WAM) School in Freetown received education scholarships under my supervision to study in Bournemouth, UK—without discrimination, which was unknown to me in my country.

Upon my second return to the UK, I studied again at ICM, Bournemouth University, Sunderland University, University of Abertay Dundee in Scotland, University of Keele, University of St Mark & St John (Marjon University in Plymouth), and Brunel University in London, where I was researching for a doctorate degree (EdD) until I suffered a stroke while writing this book. I also completed the PGCE to obtain formal teaching qualifications accepted in UK educational institutions and earned an MA in Education. When I recover, I intend to continue my EdD research where I left off.

Thus, tribalism and political discrimination against being born a Mende from Kenema and an SLPP supporter have opened doors to education at the world stage, beyond control of the All Peoples' Congress (APC). No APC politician can deny this fact but must bow to respect how God controls every human being's destiny, regardless of wealth or political affiliation.

When I submitted the Education Policy Document to President Julious Maada Bio in London, only almighty God oversaw the implementation of FREE QUALITY EDUCATIONAL FOUNDATIONS benefiting poor people and their children in Sierra Leone for our country's future.

Benefits today are for tomorrow. This was the APC policy I chiefly challenged and changed from:

"EDUCATION IS A PRIVILEGE IN SIERRA LEONE, AND THOSE WHO CAN AFFORD IT CAN ACHIEVE AS MANY QUALIFICATIONS AS POSSIBLE, EVEN ABROAD. ACQUIRING EDUCATIONAL QUALIFICATIONS SHOULD NOT BE THE GOVERNMENT'S RESPONSIBILITY BUT THE INDIVIDUAL'S."

To

"EDUCATION IN SIERRA LEONE IS A BASIC HUMAN RIGHT FOR ALL SIERRA LEONEANS, WHETHER RICH OR POOR. ALL CHILDREN MUST HAVE ACCESS TO FREE QUALITY EDUCATION."

Educational support that once denied the poor, especially in provinces due to political affiliations, is no longer in existence or constitutional. It no longer matters which political party a child's parents support; the policy covers all children growing up in the country.

God bless President Julious Maada Bio for prioritizing the poor and education. May his agenda continue reign for answering our cries. The benefits of FREE QUALITY EDUCATION are for future years when trained professionals serve the country. APC leaders will be held accountable for misusing natural resources with no benefit to poor farmers left behind.

In the poor farming environment, skepticism grows about the rich seen locally only during election campaigns hugging babies for votes. Most are not respected or relied upon for government assistance.

Some politicians now use "swear blood" tactics to confirm votes, but farmers feign acceptance then disappoint such politicians, identifying them as "agents of Satan." We avoid them, voting for those who care about us and our children's future.

Humans know themselves best and what they enjoy most. I enjoy working with people, young or adult, and investigating how they understand and enjoy their work.

That is why I love teaching more than all other jobs. Professionally, I am a Business Studies teacher for GCSE in secondary academy schools, and BTEC for HNC/D Pearson qualifications in sixth-forms and further education colleges in London's education system.

CURRENT SENSITIVE POLITICAL ISSUES IN OUR SLPP GOVERNMENT – THE NEW CHAIRMAN SHOULD BE AWARE OF:

Social media now effectively spreads loud messages globally. Ngor Joe can speak his mind alone on social media, even from his coffee farm in the Eastern Province, with only a mobile phone and discuss political drama that embarrassed our First Lady in parliament at Tower Hill, Freetown, uninterrupted. Only the First Lady can counteract later, claiming MPs were having lunchtime fun and their childish behaviour was not the political issues meant to be discussed. "If my COCOA BORN NA-FIRE, there is nothing wrong when I get held up gossiping about the SLPP Chairmanship election." Social media messages just make me laugh!

A few weeks ago, the SLPP demonstrated a truly DEMOCRATIC election process for their new chairman at Bintumani Hotel. It was one of the most pleasurable events I have seen in video. I saw the First Lady dancing behind President Maada Bio, who was focused on his dancing—bowing and standing upright before speaking. He made clear that the SLPP chairman election follows the founders' democratic process and named them individually.

President Bio warned delegates authorized to vote to do so freely without intimidation. The First Lady sat separately, busy on phone calls in clearly tormented positions, perhaps because plans went unexpectedly.

The jubilation at Bintumani could not compare with the friendly jokes shared between President Robert Mugabe of Zimbabwe and me at coffee in the OAU conference hall during his first international visit to Sierra Leone in 1980.

Finally, Sir Jimmy Batilo Songa won as National Chairman with 618 votes, beating Engineer Amara Jambai Konneh who got 396 votes.

This began another political saga within the SLPP, clearly involving our First Lady Mrs. Fatima Jabbie-Bio.

Her unrest that day appeared due to her spiritual confusion from supporting SLPP while Sir Songa's win blocked her plans to undermine SLPP internally. Sir Songa now leads, and the First Lady cannot control SLPP affairs internally.

Her body language supports my psychological reading that Fatima Jabbie-Bio was a time bomb planted in SLPP by the APC opposition through marriage, set to explode unexpectedly, possibly endangering President Julious Maada Bio's life.

To prove this, consider the tight relationship and stalking of President Maada Bio inside and outside the country. Such secretive love cannot stay hidden under the clothes of any former fake actress like Fatima formerly with Nollywood.

While we have no authority over their marriage, we pray they remain husband and wife even if President Bio retires as president in 2028.

It now seems Fatima proposed marriage seeing Maada as an opportunity to plant a long-time political seed in Sierra Leone.

She failed to understand the political requirements in Sierra Leone—such as "what qualifies anyone to genuinely be a politician here."

Without those qualifications, our First Lady Fatima Bio suddenly declares on social media her intention to continue President Bio's role after his retirement, claiming the presidency they fought for "will remain their own property, as a father has the right to pass his property to his family."

This is her current headache, but is she troubled by any other issues or excessive makeup? We have the right to worry; after all, she is our brother's wife.

Another issue is the admiration from APC party members and supporters witnessing SLPP's internal jubilation electing Sir Jimmy Batilo Songa National Chairman.

This jubilation spread from Sierra Leone to the UK, USA, and many countries worldwide.

Could Sir Jimmy become our next president if he becomes SLPP's flagbearer for the 2028 election?

On 20 October 2025, in Freetown, the official handover of National Chairmanship from Dr. Prince Harding to Sir Jimmy was held amidst jubilation.

Sir Jimmy warmly welcomed all stakeholders, particularly security forces protecting lives and property. He warned that SLPP government fully controls military and police and pledged to further the government's agenda strictly to ensure all lives remain safe.

THE POLITICAL ADDRESS SPEECHES OF SIR JIMMY BATILO SONGA

This is the portion of Sir Jimmy's address to the congregation that the APC political party has written a lengthy petition about and spread throughout the country. They claim that the new chairman has started threatening the public, creating unease among the population. However, Sir Jimmy is bold and committed to speaking the truth, which benefits everyone in this country, especially now that he is National Chairman of the SLPP. If the APC is frightened and nervous of Batilo's presence, they must consider that they are also safe under the SLPP government.

Sir Jimmy Batilo Songa's speech on 20 October 2025 in Freetown not only demonstrated his fearlessness toward the APC but also alerted APC leaders that he is fully aware of their current tactics, including their corrupt dealings with security forces, such as the army and police. Consequently, they have turned to social media to communicate directly with grassroots voters, who can access information anytime via their mobile phones.

Some respected APC members have joined illiterate social media users posting interviews and fake publicity claiming President Maada Bio is responsible for drug cartels causing illnesses and thousands of deaths of young university students and graduates almost daily.

It is unfortunate to see some women feigning distress on social media and blaming the government for their personal misfortunes. Do they expect any sensible person to heed such negative APC propaganda?

What all Sierra Leoneans want from our government is focus on welfare, considering:

i. Sufficient good food daily,

ii. Health and medical facilities nationwide,

iii. Education for children throughout the country,

iv. Transportation infrastructure, noting that railway transport was removed by APC's Siaka Stevens due to political grudges against the Eastern province, particularly Kailahun District, impeding transport of cash crops to Freetown for export,

v. Stability of our currency to facilitate purchasing power parity in international markets.

Clearly, the country is manageable if the ruling party pays attention and effectively provides these amenities.

My question is: What can the APC show on record that they provided while in office since the days of Siaka Stevens in 1967? One of his legacies is the death penalty by hanging at Pademba Road Prison. If the country has enemies, are they not the founders of the APC party, whose policies remain deeply rooted?

Since SLPP assumed power on 14 April 2018 under President Julious Maada Bio, Sierra Leoneans have witnessed positive political changes including:

i. Upgrading of motor roads,

ii. Construction of motor road bridges to link communities,

iii. Introduction of FREE QUALITY EDUCATION policy—from nursery to secondary level—allowing all children in Sierra Leone, including non-nationals with foreign parents, access to basic education,

iv. Increased efforts to enhance farming and food production, reducing hunger and supporting farmers,

v. Introduction of “Keke” and “Waka-Fine” motorcycle and bus transport systems easing transport in Freetown and other key areas,

vi. Efforts to provide special transportation for schoolchildren, compensating for abandonment of railway transport in 1967 by Siaka Stevens, facilitating timely school attendance and enabling education policy success.

Therefore, social media politicians criticizing President Bio’s SLPP government should stop, as many current facilities owe to his dynamic leadership and cannot be ignored in a rush to restore APC control through democratic voting in Sierra Leone as per our political structure.

My observation of APC dates back to 1964, when President Bio was a baby.

They seek power only to destroy what SLPP has built through sacrifice and envy of its values, including first Prime Minister Sir Milton Margai, a Mende by tribe.

This roots APC members' ignorance globally. Without understanding the country, its people's will, and knowledge to provide, any Sierra Leonean attempting politics will live in frustration. Are these people truly ignorant of their senses?

As a son of poor Eastern province farmers, educated and living in London, I know what I write about—the realities in Sierra Leone. I tried my best living in Freetown, attending Methodist Boys' High School under my uncle's care. Watching parliamentary debates tempted me toward politics, influenced by Hon. Mana Kpaka's criticisms of often-sleeping PC Jaiah Kikai.

I write not to enter politics but to educate politicians, especially APC, who regard Mende people as backward and tribalistic. The Mende's strength lies in understanding what is required. Only human knowledge enlightens anyone on their duties. Curiosity to acquire this knowledge is a Mende gift.

Mende spend ample time seeking detailed understanding to avoid future embarrassment, though often accused of wasting time. They ask fundamental questions about progress to calculate outcomes and alternatives. Is there harm in such curiosity?

Mende approach politics differently than others, refusing to tolerate unchecked government project abuses. Other tribes accept governments funds flowing into personal offshore accounts.

We are fed up with APC and wish to uphold honesty and teamwork in politics, considering voters' wishes nationally, following the motto: ONE COUNTRY, ONE PEOPLE—ONE PEOPLE, ONE COUNTRY.

DUAL NATIONALITY STATUS WITH SIERRA LEONE ("Two-Seems" Card) HOLDERS:

If President Julius Maada Bio seriously meddles with "Two-Seems" to favor friends without constitutional amendments, extending such favors to aspiring politicians bypassing due process, it risks his political downfall.

Sierra Leonean nationals with dual citizenship should have other citizenships revoked, return, live five consecutive years in Sierra Leone before contesting politics. As an SLPP member since 1964, I dislike favoritism and discrimination within our party. No one is above Sierra Leone's laws governing political conduct.

When Mr. Tamba Lamina was High Commissioner in London, I met him and Deputy High Commissioner, late Agnes Macauley, in 2019. I raised the "Two-Seems" issue, and was advised it was too early to discuss with the president, recommending patience for him to settle before tackling it.

While constitutions are amendable, we support the "Two-Seems" provision as it protects genuine Sierra Leoneans from exploitation by so-called educated elites abroad, some holding forged qualifications. Until a thorough debate and formal parliamentary amendment, "Two-Seems" remains non-negotiable. No one, not even the president, is above Sierra Leone's laws.

NO ONE IS ABOVE THE LAW OF SIERRA LEONE, EVEN THE PRESIDENT.

(2). The Present

2017: Change of Government: From APC to SLPP.

On 31 March 2018, a change of government took place in Sierra Leone: from the All Peoples Congress (APC) political party rule to the Sierra Leone Peoples Party (SLPP) rule. Julius Maada Bio assumed the highest office in the land—the State House—and became President of Sierra Leone during a presidential run-off against Samura Kamara, the APC presidential candidate. Julius Maada Bio of the SLPP secured 51.8% of the vote, while Samura Kamara of the APC received 48.2%, a narrow margin of 3.6%. This slender victory over the APC, which was reluctant to concede power, was indeed "a very painful and bitter pill to swallow," but it was "God's answered prayer" for the people of Sierra Leone who stood firm for change. Indeed, that was when most people realized that "God is greater than politics!" Julius Maada Bio's political victory did not come as a surprise. He had worked patiently and diligently for a long time, planting the idea in voters' hearts that he would be a reliable democratic choice for president. His mindset for becoming president developed from within and without harming anyone. The circumstances that shaped President Julius Maada Bio's political path in Sierra Leone—whether recognized or not—did not arise from a "Nyamjodo-Arabic Murrayman spell from The Gambia," as some attribute. What is responsible for his success can be summarized as follows:

Therefore, voters had made up their minds at the time of the 2018 run-off with Samora the land—the State House—and became President of Sierra Leone during a presidential run-off against Samura Kamara, the APC presidential candidate. Julius Maada Bio of the SLPP secured 51.8% of the vote, while Samura

For reasons that he was earlier on among those young soldiers including Valentine Strasser who paid a visit to President J.S. Momoh during the Easy-Ride military takeover in 1992 and the group jointly agreed to let Valentine Strasser lead.

In 1996 he staged a palace coup on Valentine Strasser because of delaying the military junta government for allowing the proposed civilian general election, in that same year (1996) he called a meeting of all registered political parties in Sierra Leone at the Bintumani Conference during which he proposed to appoint the political leaders of each of the political parties and this time, Mr Ahmad Tejan Kabbah, who was retiring from the United Nations as international civil servant won among those vied to lead the SLPP, including lawyer Charles Margai and was the presidential candidate to represent the SLPP.

A General Election was allowed that year according to national agreement under the watch of Maada Bio who was the Head of State and at that brief time, he was able to oversee the transition of the military junta government to a democratic civilian government in Sierra Lone that we are all still witnessing. Therefore, Maada Bio opened the gateway for a breathing space for all political aspirants in Sierra Leone. This occurrence of political approach that banned the APC's "single party democracy" to multiparty democracy which allowed civilians the voting right to which ever political party of their choice made Julius Maada Bio very popular, as a genuine modern politician of the day. He led the way to everyone's political aspirations in Sierra Leone.

Kamara that Maada Bio was their right choice at that right strategic time.

"As patient dog always eats the fattest bone," that is what Maada Bio is enjoying today, and that was one of the reasons why voters did not allow Ernest Bai Koroma a third term of presidential leadership. Indeed, President Maada Bio is teaching practical politics to all Sierra Leoneans, and members of the APC, including all political aspirants, must learn from these skills. That is what we call "education."

Although President Julius Maada Bio might have made some mistakes before, during, and after occupying the State House as the country's first gentleman, those mistakes are deemed part of his personal life and cannot interfere with his political office. It may be difficult for him to control those mistakes, and they may be embarrassing, but if the symptoms of those mistakes continue and start infecting the SLPP's core, it will be difficult for the party to win the General Election that would give Maada Bio a second term should he be chosen as Flag-Bearer in the pivotal presidential primary. His disappointment may originate even within the SLPP itself, and this reality will lay the foundation of Maada Bio's frustration, because "the Sierra Leone Peoples Party is the Sierra Leone Peoples Party and will always remain so!"

From what I learned from the late Pa Juma Sei of Kpanguima (Panguma), a market township near Kenema, when I joined the SLPP in 1964 as a toddler member—the year of current President Julius Maada Bio's birth—the SLPP is a disciplined political party, and the party's rules cannot be meddled with, especially at leadership level. The first discipline is RESPECT among members. Current members continually attempt to convince members of other parties through respect for SLPP. It is a political party to be respected and feared. It has secret investigators ready to expose members when the time comes, usually unknown until voters approach the ballot boxes, by which time bribery has ceased.

Another point of obedience is President Julius Maada Bio's stance regarding higher educational institution management. In earlier speeches, he stated that offices of Vice Chancellors in Sierra Leone's universities should become independent from the presidency, with appointments made by the university's own education professionals. What remains unclear is why he still holds the position of Vice Chancellor of the University of Sierra Leone.

Many genuine education professionals, particularly those settled or engaged in Sierra Leone's education sector or other professions unrelated to politics, deserve this Vice Chancellor role. Politicians should not control this office. Universities worldwide, including in the UK, are centers for higher knowledge and national progress. Politicians in Sierra Leone do not prioritize this; they mostly focus on personal wealth accumulation after office, while telling us what we want to hear.

A Vice Chancellor role requires a consultant with extensive research knowledge of education and commitment to university management, expansion, and quality assessment—none of which align with politicians' interests.

Sierra Leonean academics who avoid politics would be suitable for such consultancy roles, providing motivation to settle in their home country, even post-retirement. Politicians should stay away from universities, as many never experienced university education or formal graduation. Respect for our educational institutions is overdue, and we demand it.

Many Sierra Leonean professionals in the diaspora possess professionalism capable of raising higher education management standards in Sierra Leone. Others of high repute have contributed greatly to education development. Their past contributions should not be forgotten.

PRESIDENT JULIUS MAADA BIO'S PROMISES FOR EDUCATION IN SIERRA LEONE ON HIS FIRST DAY IN OFFICE:

President Julius Maada Bio was sworn in as president representing the SLPP on 12 May 2018.

On 10 May 2018, he delivered a 40-page state opening address in Parliament, promising education reforms that excited education enthusiasts. His speech earned multiple rounds of applause as a turning point for education in Sierra Leone.

Have these promises been fulfilled since he took office?

Voters will consider this carefully in the 2023 General Elections. Whoever occupies the State House must prioritize the nation's interests, refraining from personal gain to continuously deliver benefits for all, especially Sierra Leoneans.

The key questions are:

Has President Julius Maada Bio delivered on his education promises made on 10 May 2018, or have political diversions led to different outcomes? Are these promises beneficial or otherwise to Sierra Leone?

FOCUSING ON EDUCATION IN ALL SCHOOLS:

Improving Education and Skills Training

52. The primary objective of the New Direction is to increase access to quality pre-primary, primary, secondary, technical and vocational education and training as well as university education that will enable them engage in meaningful productive economic activity. To demonstrate our commitment to education, my Government will increase and sustain budgetary allocation to education to a minimum of 20% of the national budget.

53. The change in the education system from 6-3-3-4 to 6-3-4-4 is challenging. The existing classroom blocks and teachers are not adequate to meet the needs of pupils for an additional year of schooling. This change in the educational system has also impacted on teenage pregnancy and early school leaving among girls who consider the number of years of schooling to be too many. There is no evidence to show that it has improved learning outcomes. Rather, it has imposed pressure on Government for additional classrooms and promoted teenage pregnancy. In fulfilment of my Manifesto commitment, we shall revert to the 6-3-3-4 system of education. The relevant authorities will advise when it will be best for this change to be effective. To improve on the system, My Government intends to increase contact hours, build additional classrooms, eliminate the two shift system and develop technical and vocational education.

54. Mr. Speaker, Honourable Members, I am pleased to officially pronounce that effective next academic year starting September 2018, my Government will introduce Free Education from primary level to senior secondary school as promised. I have already engaged many of our partners for support of this programme and I am pleased to report that, our international and donor partners have expressed commitments to support my administration. To ensure effective coordination of support of this programme, Government will establish a Multi-Partner Education for Development Basket Fund. In support of this, two Committees will be established. First, a High Level Inter-Ministerial and Partners Group (IMPG) on Free Education comprising of relevant ministries and partners will be set up. This Group will provide the strategic guidance to the planning and design of the programme, mobilise resources and oversee the implementation. Second, a Technical Group (TG) on Education comprising professionals from the relevant MDAs and partner agencies will be established to design the programme, coordinate and monitor the implementation. The Technical Group will report to the High Level Inter Ministerial and Partners Group.

55. Mr. Speaker, Honourable Members, improving education governance is critical for the success of the New Direction in education. To this end, my Government will (i) review the Education Sector Plan

THE BEST TEACHER Award Scheme for the most innovative, ingenious and dedicated teachers at national and district levels (iv) provide free university education for three children of every school teacher with at least 10 years' teaching experience.

57. There is limited number of qualified teachers at all levels. Only 55 percent of teachers at pre-school level, 42 percent at primary level, 35 percent at Junior Secondary School, 49% at Senior Secondary School, are qualified to teach. Increasing the number of qualified teachers and ensuring fair distribution amongst districts is critical for the successful implementation of our Free Education Programme. In support of this, my administration will establish Teacher Training campuses in all districts, expand and improve on distance learning education for teachers and provide free tuition for teacher education. to ensure it is realigned with the priorities of the New Direction (ii) strengthen Education Management and Information System (EMIS) to support informed strategic decision-making (iii) develop a robust policy and legal framework for Public-Private-Partnership in the education sector (iv) develop the capacity of School Inspectorate for effective school monitoring and supervision (v) build the capacity of School Management Committees (SMC) (vi) de-politicise the Board of Governors of schools, redefine their roles, and introduce a compulsory reporting requirement (vii) respect and support the autonomy of the National Union of Students (NUSS) and (viii) promote social dialogue with relevant stakeholders in the education service delivery including the Sierra Leone Teachers Union.

56. Mr. Speaker, Honourable Members, none of us would have been here today without our greatest asset, teachers. Yet, they have been least recognized and least rewarded. This is demotivating. Let me simply state that without qualified teachers, our Free Education Programme will not be fully implemented. In the New Direction, Government will raise the morale and productivity of our teachers. To this end, I hereby pronounce a Presidential Initiative for Teachers. The Initiative will ensure that matters relating to teachers are treated with utmost importance. Additionally, my administration will (i) review and make functional the Teaching Service Commission (ii) develop a special incentive scheme for Science and French teachers as well as teachers in remote areas and those in special needs institutions (iii) introduce.

58. Mr. Speaker, Honourable Members, the amounts of public spending on fee subsidy for university education is unsustainable. Whilst we will improve on the management of the Grants-in-Aid policy, my administration will introduce Students Loan Scheme that will provide loans to deserving students to access higher education.

59. *Mr. Speaker, Free Education will increase demand for school. As a progressive Government, we need to prepare for the anticipated increase in school enrolment. Therefore, my administration will adopt a policy of One-Administrative Section-One Primary School, One-Electoral Ward-One Junior Secondary School and One-Electoral Constituency-One-Senior Secondary School. Additionally, my Government will construct new classroom blocks in urban towns to reduce congestion in schools and eventually eliminate the two-shift system in the next few years.*

60. *To sustain high school enrolment and improve learning, my administration will work with World Food Programme and other food agencies as well as the Ministry of Agriculture and Forestry to expand school feeding programmes in all public assisted primary schools.*

61. *The cost of transportation constitutes a major share of urban household expenditure on education. This high cost of urban transportation causes lateness and affect school attendance which further affect learning. My Government will re-introduce school bus system in large urban towns on a cost recovery basis and less than the prevailing market price.*

62. Mr. Speaker, Honourable Members, the high level of adult illiteracy in Sierra Leone estimated at 60 percent is unacceptable in any progressive nation. As part of my commitment to education, my administration will work with partners to develop and implement cost effective strategies for providing basic literacy and numeracy training for our adults who were not fortunate to attend school. Some of these will include (i) initially establishing one functional adult literacy centre in every district and later expanding to every chiefdom using existing school facilities and (ii) integrating literacy programmes into agricultural and livelihood programmes.

63. The New Direction believes that training is the foundation for enhancing the country's competitiveness. To this end, my Government will (i) review and standardise the curriculum and certification for Technical and Vocational Education and Training (TVET) (ii) develop a national apprenticeship scheme which can provide internship for trainees of TVET institutes and at the same time provide direct training for youth and (iii) develop a robust Public-Private-Partnership framework to increase private sector participation in TVET training. Also, my Government will establish in every district capital one Polytechnic Institution that will be fully equipped with modern tools and equipment for technical vocational education and training in areas with high potential for job creation among the population.

64. Mr. Speaker, the conditions of our institutions of higher learning and in particular the citadel of knowledge, University of Sierra Leone and Njala University are deplorable. We have lost the glory of being the Athens of West Africa. We require urgent actions to develop our Universities and all other higher institutions. Already, my Government has created a separate Ministry of Technical and Higher Education that will solely focus on technical and higher education. My intention is to establish a university system that employs its own leadership as chancellors and Vice Chancellors with distinguished and proven records of higher education leadership and significant international clout and contacts (funding and research networks). In this light, effective 2019, I as President will cease to be the Chancellor of the University of Sierra Leone. In the coming months, the 2005 Universities Act will be reviewed to reflect this and many other changes where necessary.

65. Science and Technology is the bedrock for the development of any modern economy. Unfortunately, in Sierra Leone, the schools and colleges lack even the basic facilities for scientific research. My Government is setting up a Directorate for Science, Technology and Innovation to develop a framework for scientific research. Initially, this Directorate will be midwifed in the Office of the President but shall work closely with the Ministry of Technical and Higher Education. 17 66. Mr. Speaker, Honourable Members, one of the reasons for attitudinal challenges is limited civic education.

This is compounded by mass illiteracy among the population. If we are to develop as a nation, we must educate our people on rights, responsibilities and obligations as good citizens. To this end, my Government will launch a National Civic Education Programme to provide civic education in our educational institutions and communities. Additionally, my administration will direct that civics be re-introduced in our schools and colleges, comprehensive curriculum for all levels will be developed and civic educators be provided training to cascade the training in schools.

to ensure it is realigned with the priorities of the New Direction (ii) strengthen Education Management and Information System (EMIS) to support informed strategic decision-making (iii) develop a robust policy and legal framework for Public-Private-Partnership in the education sector (iv) develop the capacity of School Inspectorate for effective school monitoring and supervision (v) build the capacity of School Management Committees (SMC) (vi) de-politicise the Board of Governors of schools, redefine their roles, and introduce a compulsory reporting requirement (vii) respect and support the autonomy of the National Union of Students (NUSS) and (viii) promote social dialogue with relevant stakeholders in the education service delivery including the Sierra Leone Teachers Union.

56. Mr. Speaker, Honourable Members, none of us would have been here today without our greatest asset, teachers. Yet, they have been least recognized and least rewarded. This is demotivating. Let me simply state that without qualified teachers, our Free Education Programme will not be fully implemented. In the New Direction, Government will raise the morale and productivity of our teachers. To this end, I hereby pronounce a Presidential Initiative for Teachers. The Initiative will ensure that matters relating to teachers are treated with utmost importance. Additionally, my administration will (i) review and make functional the Teaching Service Commission (ii) develop a special incentive scheme for Science and French teachers as well as teachers in remote areas and those in special needs institutions (iii) introduce.

LOCATION FOR ACCREDITED UNIVERSITIES IN SIERRA LEONE:

Let me briefly elaborate on the location of accredited university educational institutions in Sierra Leone and explain the effects these higher education institutions have on their local areas and the country at large.

Universities worldwide are meant to provide higher education opportunities for talented individuals to improve their learning, primarily through research, to contribute to existing knowledge under the supervision of appointed and approved university professors.

For any institution to publicly call itself a university, it must have officially approved facilities capable of delivering university education that meets global knowledge standards.

The word "university" derives from "universe," meaning the whole world. In some countries, certain university qualifications are worthless and such institutions are labeled "degree mills." I don't believe such universities are needed in Sierra Leone. Although private universities have been emerging worldwide, such as in the US, it is crucial that Sierra Leone's government establish assessment bodies to vet institutions aspiring to become universities.

The University Court of the University of Sierra Leone is an internationally respected body suited for this role, as it is not political. Otherwise, Sierra Leoneans studying at commercially driven institutions will be disappointed when seeking further education or international employment, where university qualifications undergo rigorous authentication.

Fourah Bay College and Njala University College are internationally recognized and accredited by the University Court of Sierra Leone. Their Bachelor's, Master's, Doctorate degrees, certificates, and diplomas are valid for use within Sierra Leone and beyond.

Many universities have recently emerged in Sierra Leone. Universities established primarily as commercial ventures by foreign investors exploit the eagerness of young learners. Graduates often receive "qualifications" that hold no real value beyond the paper they are printed on. Sierra Leoneans should be alert to these practices before it is too late to address them.

Educational Foundation Years – BASIC EDUCATION (Children need high levels of nutritional support at these stages):

i. Early Years (Under-5s) or Nursery School Level

ii. Primary School Level

iii. Secondary School Level (Children can withstand hunger longer at this level)

Further Education (Adolescence and young adult years):

iv. Sixth-Form Level (Preparatory stage for Higher Education)

v. Vocational/Technical Education (Certificate & Diploma) Level

Higher Education:

vi. University Education (First degree/graduate – Bachelor's) Level

vii. Postgraduate Level (Master's)

viii. Doctorate Level – (1) Academic Doctorate (2) Professional Doctorate: usually research-based under university supervision during an agreed period.

Levels one to three (Nursery, Primary, Secondary School) are the preparatory or foundation years of learning. These are the most important learning stages worldwide, as future foundations are built here. This segment is categorically "Basic Education." It must be strong in any country due to the associated long-term advantages.

In the UK, educational qualifications are recognized according to the Regulated Qualifications Framework (RQF), monitored in England, Wales, and Northern Ireland, which identifies 9 levels of qualifications.

Entry level

Each entry level qualification is available at three sub-levels - 1, 2 and 3. Entry level 3 is the most difficult.

Entry level qualifications are:

- entry level award
- entry level certificate (ELC)
- entry level diploma
- entry level English for speakers of other languages (ESOL)
- entry level essential skills
- entry level functional skills
- Skills for Life

Level 1

Level 1 qualifications are:

- first certificate
- GCSE - grades 3, 2, 1 or grades D, E, F, G
- level 1 award
- level 1 certificate
- level 1 diploma
- level 1 ESOL
- level 1 essential skills
- level 1 functional skills
- level 1 national vocational qualification (NVQ)
- music grades 1, 2 and 3

Level 2

Level 2 qualifications are:

- CSE - grade 1
- GCSE - grades 9, 8, 7, 6, 5, 4 or grades A*, A, B, C
- intermediate apprenticeship
- level 2 award
- level 2 certificate
- level 2 diploma
- level 2 ESOL
- level 2 essential skills
- level 2 functional skills
- level 2 national certificate
- level 2 national diploma
- level 2 NVQ
- music grades 4 and 5
- O level - grade A, B or C

Level 3

Level 3 qualifications are:

- A level
- access to higher education diploma
- advanced apprenticeship
- applied general
- AS level
- international Baccalaureate diploma
- level 3 award
- level 3 certificate

- level 3 diploma
- level 3 ESOL
- level 3 national certificate
- level 3 national diploma
- level 3 NVQ
- music grades 6, 7 and 8
- tech level

Level 4

Level 4 qualifications are:

- certificate of higher education (CertHE)
- higher apprenticeship
- higher national certificate (HNC)
- level 4 award
- level 4 certificate
- level 4 diploma
- level 4 NVQ

Level 5

Level 5 qualifications are:

- diploma of higher education (DipHE)
- foundation degree
- higher national diploma (HND)
- level 5 award
- level 5 certificate
- level 5 diploma
- level 5 NVQ

Level 6

Level 6 qualifications are:

- degree apprenticeship
- degree with honours - for example bachelor of the arts (BA) hons, bachelor of science (BSc) hons
- graduate certificate
- graduate diploma
- level 6 award
- level 6 certificate
- level 6 diploma
- level 6 NVQ
- ordinary degree without honours

Level 7

Level 7 qualifications are:

- integrated master's degree, for example Master of Engineering (MEng)
- level 7 award
- level 7 certificate
- level 7 diploma
- level 7 NVQ
- master's degree, for example Master of Arts (MA), Master of Science (MSc)
- postgraduate certificate
- postgraduate certificate in education (PGCE)
- postgraduate diploma

Level 8

Level 8 qualifications are:

- doctorate, for example, Doctor of Philosophy (PhD or DPhil, EdD)
- level 8 award
- level 8 certificate
- level 8 diploma

Higher Education: Higher educational institutions are institutions engaged in providing knowledge, commonly referred to as universities. Employers are ready to pay high salaries to those with qualifications from universities for several reasons. Secondly, great leaders don't accept the status quo; they accept challenges that are overcome through university learning. These challenges are known only when one completes a university education at a standard level in their chosen field. How can students be prepared better for the workforce? How can education adapt to emerging technology and modern faculty administration dynamics?

Those pursuing academic research at the Doctorate degree level in a renowned university in the UK address today's big questions in higher education and embody reflective, future leadership.

A Doctor of Education (EdD) can provide learners with the leadership abilities and perspective to meet the challenges of today and tomorrow. Explore higher education focused on leadership theory and develop the expertise to apply it in real-world situations. Build a contemporary understanding of administrative relationships and the student experience.

Gain actionable insight into higher education governance, policy, and financing to help effect institutional change.

Holders of the EdD professional degree are practicing education professionals who have the opportunity to observe first-hand the issues and sometimes shortcomings their institutions face daily. This knowledge and experience create increased opportunities for education professionals. Higher learning institutions in the UK that provide educational knowledge at level 8 are always seeking innovators eager to strengthen curricula, employ emerging technologies, and improve the delivery and efficiency of higher education courses.

What are PhD and EdD?

The difference between the PhD (Education) and EdD qualifications is that the latter is a professional qualification at the doctoral level, oriented toward professionals who want to leverage educational leadership skills. Combining both research and application, the EdD is applicable to a broad range of industries inside and outside the world of education. In other words, this degree aims to create highly experienced educators who want to bring productive changes to organisations where graduates are hired to produce, with corresponding high salaries.

PhD (Education) means Doctor of Philosophy in Education, which is recognized as the highest level of academic qualification in the field of education, including specialties such as medicine or law. This qualification prepares candidates for a specific research area over 3-6 years, during which they learn to present discoveries. The process also improves teaching abilities and the explanation of projects in various circumstances. PhD researchers learn to identify gaps in existing research, interpret relevant literature contextually, propose new hypotheses, and conduct original research. The PhD research focuses more on academic discoveries and theories that have been published, whereas EdD research emphasizes practical or professional experience gained in different locations over time.

The commonality is that both doctorate degrees require a research thesis following the university's regulations, supervised by the researcher's advisor. The final examination is the thesis defence, known as the "Viva-voce," a Latin expression for questions and answers about the thesis. Doctoral research aims to discover additional knowledge, with new research continually emerging and adding to existing knowledge.

All universities in all countries receive DOCTORATE awarding authorization first (such as from the university court, institute, or ministry of education) before accepting researchers to pursue this level, even if staff are qualified to supervise. Such authorization must be displayed at strategic public locations on university premises, such as in the offices of the Principal and Vice Chancellor.

The PhD (Education) degree yields many benefits for those who complete it in accredited universities, such as those in the United Kingdom:

The PhD lends credibility in education, expertise, and social mobility.

PhD students enhance their research skills and gain technical expertise.

It gives students the opportunity to conduct research in an area of personal interest, making discoveries and contributing to knowledge.

University education should be considered with specific care, which readers of this book must take seriously, because university education should not be used as a political achievement or campaign platform. Educational qualifications at all levels are meant to generate specific benefits for the holders. Many problems in Africa today originate from educated people, and these problems vary in reasons, including tribalism, political party affiliations, sectionalism, and sexism.

For Sierra Leone communities, it is not good when people graduate with Bachelor's or Master's degrees in various fields without achieving their goals.

When students attend university, their expectations vary, such as earning millions of Leones, surpassing the combined income of Mr. and Mrs. Blaa, riding in the first Mercedes Benz, and building their first houses in upscale areas like Wilkinson Road, Spur Road, or in the mountains near President Maada Bio's house.

When such graduates do not get their dream jobs immediately after graduation, they become disappointed and may develop negative habits leading to unnecessary problems. Do you go to university to graduate and run yourself into trouble? Why are these problems happening? Some occur because graduates lack the skills to create or sell products to earn money. They also lack the skills to create jobs for themselves and others. These are some of the challenges facing university graduates in African countries today.

It is necessary to maintain some vocational/technical institutions locally. A learning institution such as the Eastern

Polytechnic in Kenema is ideal rather than merely pursuing a university in that area.
This is because vocational institutions train learners to use their hands and minds to make products to earn money. Vocational graduates are skilled enough to make items to sell and earn a living. When their handiwork becomes highly demanded, surpassing their production capacity, they can employ and train others interested in working with them. They easily become entrepreneurs and create small businesses that establish employment to create jobs for others.
Governments should provide more facilities for learners in vocational institutions rather than focusing solely on universities where graduates expect government (civil service) employment after graduation.
Vocationally talented young people have the potential to pay more taxes depending on how many people they employ, contributing tax revenue to the government. This is more reasonable to consider than producing more university graduates who look forward to government jobs, where some may engage in corrupt practices like stealing government funds and leftover supplies.
If young people in Kenema or other areas have the necessary talents to pursue university degrees, my advice is to apply and study hard to achieve the qualifications they want. University qualifications are excellent and in demand worldwide. I mention Kenema because I originate from the Koya Chiefdom in Kenema District, a Mende-Mende settlement with extended family in Dama, Tonkia, Gaura, Pujehun, Nongowa, Dodo, Gorama Mende, Kandu Lepiama,

Langurama Ya, Lower Bambara, and other chiefdoms in Kailahun and Kono Districts.

I am particularly interested in the development of young people in this area, although the whole of Sierra Leone is also important. As mentioned earlier about the backwardness of education in Sierra Leone, I emphasize that the Northern Province has not only lagged but remains COMPLETELY ASLEEP regarding education. Politicians there believe educating youth empowers them to stand against existing political powers—as per the thoughts of Siaka Stevens. Although Stevens died on 29 May 1988, his political legacy lives on among APC followers in the Northern Province, many of whom still uphold his philosophy unquestioningly. This backward thinking has developed into chronic issues affecting not only the Northern Province but the entire country. It is honest to say the political problems in Sierra Leone originate from the Northern Province, the base of the APC party.

The most valuable asset parents encourage their children to pursue in this area is petty street trading from door to door (without formal education). By age 15, many girls have two or three children with different fathers, unsure of their biological paternity.

I do not believe this is a decent way of life, and politicians must strictly address these conditions for the benefit of future generations.

Politicians from this area are aware of this behaviour but ignore it as long as the youth do not oppose their political power. Therefore, the Northern Province continues to suffer damage, perpetuated by politicians representing their constituencies in the National Parliament at Tower Hill,

Freetown. Political representatives who do not encourage education among their youth are as ineffective as having no representation at all.

Finally, when educational institutions are established in any location within a country, their effectiveness becomes paramount, especially when the marketability of their courses is widely recognized by learners in relevant fields. As the world progresses with varying human needs, the courses offered must align with the demands of global job and employment markets, not only in Sierra Leone. Educated individuals with relevant qualifications are prioritized for employment opportunities. Young people need proper preparation through education to successfully enter the job market.

Employment markets today are highly saturated and competitive, with developed Western welfare countries also struggling to maintain economic control. Achieving educational success now requires dedicated time to develop personal talents that help ensure future survival and prosperity through education.

Private educational institutions in Sierra Leone that use the name or description "UNIVERSITY" must be thoroughly inspected to ensure they meet formal criteria for university status. Institutions that do not meet these criteria should immediately cease offering and awarding degrees, as such certificates hold no value and are not recognized internationally. The Tertiary Education Commission (TEC) regulates the establishment and accreditation of universities in Sierra Leone. Only universities accredited by the TEC should be recognized by the public, which currently includes institutions such as the University of Makeni, Limkokwing

University of Creative Technology, University of Management & Technology (UNIMTECH), and United Methodist University (UMU), among others. The public is advised to avoid unaccredited institutions to protect their educational and professional futures.

If universities are politically motivated, education enthusiasts must understand that education cannot be politicized to create false awareness in communities or the country. Politics in Sierra Leone has infiltrated all aspects of life, hindering individual growth and causing further instability.

Respect has been shown to President Julius Maada Bio and his wife, Mrs. Fatima Jabbie-Bio; however, recent revelations about her conduct have caused concern. It appears Fatima Bio has sought to leverage Maada Bio's popularity for personal political gain, attempting to claim the presidency through marriage, which conflicts with the constitutional processes of leadership selection in Sierra Leone.

Marriage to a president does not make the presidency family property. While the marriage should be respected and hoped to endure after President Maada Bio's tenure, Fatima Bio's behavior has been likened to overstepping appropriate boundaries and requires correction. She has been active politically but without formal appointment, and her ambitions should not interfere with national governance or political party ownership, which belongs equally to all Sierra Leoneans.

Fatima Bio has crossed a political red line, and her understanding of democratic politics in Sierra Leone is questioned. It has been suggested she might better pursue political ambitions in her birth country, The Gambia, rather than Sierra Leone. Her conduct is seen as disrespectful to Sierra Leone's political customs and citizens and is a cause for serious concern.

Politicians are expected to expand job markets primarily through vocational training and sponsorship, not through divisive political maneuvers. Fatima Bio's conduct distracts from economic development efforts and job creation initiatives.

INTERNATIONAL-FOREIGN INVESTORS (IFIs)

International-Foreign Investors (IFIs) are affluent business organizations from wealthy countries seeking new markets in developing countries like Sierra Leone. Their interest lies in expanding market possibilities as their home countries face saturated or highly competitive business environments. Early entry into new markets allows these organizations to establish themselves, understand customer demands, and provide tailored services.

IFIs are motivated primarily by profit rather than genuine interest in the countries' landscapes, cultures, or people. They exploit gaps caused by a lack of skilled and educated personnel in developing countries.

Politicians are keen to attract IFIs because their investments create jobs for the local educated and skilled workforce, which typically requires at least two years of relevant experience and proper educational qualifications. IFIs do not fill vacancies with unqualified applicants but prioritize merit, regardless of political affiliation.

Jobs created by IFIs serve the interests of all qualified citizens, not only political supporters, and are often highlighted by politicians as evidence of good governance before elections. Hence, citizens are advised to pursue education continuously to qualify for such employment opportunities rather than rely exclusively on government jobs. Sustained education and skills development remain critical for obtaining meaningful employment and driving economic growth in Sierra Leone

The behavior of politicians who work hard to attract International-Foreign Investors (IFIs) into developing countries like Sierra Leone is often welcomed by local voters due to the job creation that results. However, caution is necessary regarding the types of businesses these IFIs introduce and the jobs they create. The core question is whether Sierra Leone wants quick job creation or long-term human development for its youth. Governments should prioritize IFIs that focus on human resource development, especially for young people, because once IFIs withdraw, local workers may lose their jobs despite the profits made using cheap local labor under government agreements.

Governments should critically assess the benefits provided by IFIs beyond annual profit contributions. This includes infrastructure improvements like roads and electricity in local communities where IFIs operate. Concerns exist about whether politicians prioritize community development or merely accumulate wealth, neglecting local welfare. Agreements with IFIs must be transparent and include provisions for local workforce training. Common practices, such as bringing mostly foreign staff and employing few locals, as sometimes seen with Chinese IFIs, should be scrutinized.

Drawing on the Indonesian experience with the Korindo palm oil project in West Papua, the establishment of IFIs can severely affect indigenous populations when land and resources are taken without proper consultation or benefit-sharing. The Korindo project devastated tribal communities by taking their lands and forests, leaving them without livelihood and representation in negotiations. This case highlights the importance for Sierra Leone to carefully investigate IFIs' operations, local land use, and long-term impacts.

Beyond job creation, IFIs should generate spillover benefits for uneducated citizens who cannot secure paid employment. Many adults in Sierra Leone are illiterate yet are taxpayers and voters. Governments must ensure these populations also benefit from IFI activities, through education, infrastructure, and social services. Otherwise, there is a risk of alienating large population segments and perpetuating inequality.

Despite initiatives like free education launched by President Maada Bio, basic facilities such as clean water, hygienic sanitation, and reliable electricity are still lacking in suburban and rural schools where these programs are implemented. Agricultural communities supplying food for domestic and export markets face poor infrastructure, including bad roads and limited access to electricity, which hinders local economic development.

A cautionary note is also raised about African dependence on foreign aid, characterized as begging from former colonial powers. This dependence undermines self-reliance and allows foreign influence that can disadvantage locals. Politicians' pursuit of foreign aid without addressing long-term national development is criticized as shameful and damaging.

The concern extends to specific projects like the Chinese-funded industrial harbor in Sierra Leone, which has sparked protests due to feared environmental damage. This reflects a broader pattern where foreign investments may harm local communities and environments if not properly managed.

In conclusion, while IFIs can stimulate job creation and economic growth, Sierra Leone's government and citizens must demand transparency, equitable local benefits, sustainable development practices, and protection of indigenous rights. Balancing short-term gains with long-term human and infrastructure development is crucial for true national progress.

Black Johnson village, located 35 kilometres (22 miles) south of Freetown, Sierra Leone, is a scenic tourist attraction with black-and-gold beaches, virgin rainforests home to chimpanzees and protected bird species, and a turquoise lagoon that serves as a breeding ground for fish and turtles. However, the government recently announced plans to construct a $55 million fishing harbour and processing complex, funded by China, sparking environmental concerns among locals and conservationists.

The fisheries ministry emphasizes the project could create thousands of new jobs in impoverished communities, potentially revitalizing the local economy. Still, eco-lodge owner Tommy Gbandewa ("Tito") leads opposition on ecological grounds, fearing pollution and damage to the environment. Communities worry about the possibility of a fish-meal factory—which the government denies—due to fears of foul odors and water pollution detrimental to tourism.

The project includes modern infrastructure such as a breakwater, slipways, vessel maintenance lifts, cold storage, and fish processing factories. It aims to boost fisheries revenue from $10 million to $59 million annually, enhance export capacity with tariff-free access to the Chinese market via an Export Certification Portal, and provide sustainable livelihoods for coastal communities.

While the fisheries ministry and Chinese diplomats assure environmental protections, local residents remain cautious about the impact on their natural habitat and way of life. This tension reflects broader challenges balancing economic development ambitions with ecological conservation in Sierra Leone as the government seeks to stimulate growth while protecting its rich biodiversity.

The Black Johnson Fish Harbour Project, expected to start construction in September 2025, symbolizes a strategic partnership between Sierra Leone and China under the leadership of Presidents Maada Bio and Xi Jinping, marking a significant milestone in Sierra Leone's Blue Economy development.

DETERRING SPOOKS TO PROGRESS IN AFRICAN COUNTRIES:

Deterring Spooks are a class of powerful people in African countries who pretend to be promoting progress for their people. These power figures are African politicians, many of whom are dishonest to the people they claim to represent in their Houses of Representatives. They act as deterrents to the development of young people in African nations.

We are grateful in Sierra Leone because President Julious Maada Bio heeded advice to introduce FREE QUALITY EDUCATION in all schools. This education policy will bring lasting benefits and blessings, not immediately, but in the long term. The best parents can do is to encourage their children to take advantage of this opportunity for their future. The APC never supported such a gesture, adhering instead to the policy that "education is for those who can afford it, and the privileged may learn as much as they can." The SLPP, under President Julious Maada Bio's administration, opposes this view, affirming that "education is not a privilege but a basic human right for every child, rich or poor, to have FREE QUALITY EDUCATION before adulthood."

We thank Almighty God for this administration and hope that future leaders will continue this political agenda so that the seeds sown may grow and bear fruit for the people of Sierra Leone. Therefore, parents should not take FREE QUALITY EDUCATION lightly; the future belongs to the children who will become adults and must sustain themselves. If parents neglect this free education, they deprive their children of opportunities that will not come again.

These Deterring Spooks also manipulate foreign donations and loans from agencies like the International Monetary Fund (IMF) and World Bank to undertake grand public projects—airports, bridges, and other visible works—to buy support in elections rather than focusing on true development. The West Papua and Indonesian experiences with IFIs from South Korea, as discussed earlier, exemplify these dynamics. Such loans place African countries in indebtedness that future governments must repay, often without benefiting the people.

Therefore, I assert as an African national and Sierra Leonean that Deterring Spooks—politicians who have served government roles—are obstacles to the country's progress. Their strategy is to provide mere lip service, claiming involvement in beneficial yet unrealized projects, rather than delivering real development.

WHAT DO WE WANT IN SIERRA LEONE FROM OUR POLITICIANS?

i. We are not slaves and have not been since our country was declared “a freedom zone of the world when that ship arrived on 10 May 1787 with 380 free black slaves in a location called Frenchman’s Bay.” Since then, the capital city was founded and called "FREETOWN", the city of the world's freedom.

ii. We are now in the 21st Century, and yet we still beg for our basic human needs—food, clothing, and shelter—for survival. Our politicians continue begging aid from the IMF or Western countries to sustain their existence. They take pleasure in this. Why don't they focus on educating our youth to enable them to achieve what Western countries' people have, preventing such suffering? Politicians must realize that, despite past civil war experiences, Sierra Leoneans may resort to conflict against current politics if basic needs remain unmet.

iii. We are decent human beings and Sierra Leoneans by nationality, just like the President and his cabinet. They provide meals and education for their children. So why doesn't the president ensure every primary school, including rural ones, provides daily school meals?

iv. We proudly identify as Sierra Leoneans and do not want politicians to tarnish that identity.

v. We expect politicians not to promote behaviors against human nature; we are HUMAN BEINGS.

vi. We reject politicians throwing money at crowds just to watch people fight over it and then driving away.

vii. We want an end to lies and the wasting of our human resources that leave us underdeveloped.

viii. We do not tolerate politicians wasting our money on extramarital affairs and extended families abroad.

ix. We do not expect handouts but want politicians to create conditions enabling us to feed ourselves with three square meals a day, ending hunger.

x. Sierra Leone's economic growth is challenged by macroeconomic instability, inflation pressures, and reliance on mining and agriculture. Despite projected growth of about 4.4% in 2025 and 4.8% in 2026, supported by government reforms and programs like "Feed Salone," more inclusive development focused on education, infrastructure, governance, and private sector enables sustainable progress and poverty reduction.

xi. We expect fairness from our politicians, not qualifications to exploit our humanity for personal pleasures such as having many wives, eating fine foods, traveling overseas, driving luxury cars, and using official complementary cards with the national coat of arms printed on top to summon companions at will.

xii. We want our politicians to help us learn how to provide food for ourselves by offering school meals and training facilities to acquire trades that create jobs, enabling us to support our families.

xiii. We do not want politicians to keep promoting International Foreign Investors (IFIs) who bring only short-term jobs and then leave us destitute. The enduring hunger is a root of continued conflict—"a hungry man is always an angry man ready to fight to get to eat."

xiv. Politicians should ensure daily school meals for all children, encouraging school attendance, and focus on reactivating closed schools rather than opening new ones for political propaganda.

xv. School-aged children value school meals, which help them concentrate. The Minister of Education should visit village schools to assure communities the government recognizes their talents and importance for national development.

xvi. The Education Minister should gather needs from visited schools to facilitate learning. Many talents exist in village schools but remain neglected dreams.

THE RASCALITY TRICKS OF THE INTERNATIONAL FOREIGN INVESTORS (IFIs)

Many International Foreign Investors (IFIs) operating in Sierra Leone tend to avoid offering formal "Contracts of Employment" to local workers, opting instead for "Contracts for Employment". This allows them the flexibility to terminate employment whenever they desire. Legal experts such as Lawyer HM Joko-Smart and Human Rights Commissioner Victor Idrissa Lansana can explain the differences between these contracts. Because IFIs are foreign entities, they are free to leave Sierra Leone at any time, so it is crucial for local governments to carefully evaluate the employment impacts and develop continuity plans before endorsing these investors.

IFIs typically employ local staff within close networks and provide them with operational training; however, when IFIs exit, significant employment gaps arise. The local employees left behind often face unemployment because they lack the full skills or knowledge to maintain operations independently. Governments must formulate strategies to manage these gaps effectively.

Although Sierra Leone has technical institutes and trade centers, government support for advanced training and vocational programs is insufficient. The saying "Teach the people how to fish and they will catch more fish" aptly describes the need for human development projects and vocational training. Politicians should prioritize these long-term initiatives over superficial projects like clock towers, which serve as political gestures rather than meaningful development.

Under President Julius Maada Bio's leadership, government hospitals remain in poor condition with inadequate facilities for healthcare workers. Instead of promising new state-of-the-art hospitals, efforts should focus on revitalizing existing facilities to proper standards. This neglect showcases political behavior that leaves Sierra Leone underdeveloped while politicians personally benefit by investing in mansions locally and abroad.

The public will judge political leadership based on tangible improvements in health and development, not on political propaganda. Basic needs like access to food remain a challenge in many communities; investments should focus on these essentials rather than inconsequential projects.

Sierra Leone's diamond resources are largely exploited by foreign nationals without sufficient oversight or environmental safeguards. The Kono District suffers serious environmental damage and socio-economic neglect as a result. Many locals see political appointments as their only path to livelihood, overshadowing the district's potential in agriculture, education, and talents.

The Kono people, like all Sierra Leoneans, deserve development opportunities beyond political patronage, enabling personal success and national contribution. Politics should not remain the sole route to achievement.

THE LAND TENURE SYSTEMS IN SIERRA LEONE:

Land ownership systems vary across countries as embedded within their constitutions. In Sierra Leone, especially in rural areas, our land system is primarily guided by such laws. People rely on land to survive, particularly those living in poverty. One of the key laws prohibits extending land ownership to strangers through purchase. Strangers have no right to buy land in village communities because land forms the backbone of their livelihood, supporting subsistence farming and the continued existence of Sierra Leoneans.

Strangers who settle and live among the community have the right to farm on community land but only for a limited period and solely for rotational farming use. No individual can sell a piece of land to a stranger, even for a large sum of money, and grant them ownership because the land does not belong to one person alone; it is community property belonging to present and future generations. Such a sale is prohibited as it deprives those yet unborn.

All land in the villages of the Mende community, which I am familiar with, belongs to the community collectively, not to individuals. The phrase "This is our land" is both practical and meaningful. The only action permitted is granting land to strangers living in the village for farming purposes only. A stranger cannot reside in a Mende village without being a household member under a town citizen. When a land parcel is granted to a stranger for farming, the citizen must request this land from the town chief, who then authorizes its use exclusively for farming.

All strangers must be introduced to the town chief immediately upon arrival for security reasons. This protective measure ensures that the community does not live in fear of unknown outsiders.

A stranger can live in a Mende township only if he does not develop sexual interest in the wife of any town citizen. Even admiring a Mende woman's buttocks, however nicely dressed or innocent the gesture, can spark serious conflict. Most strangers face trouble living among the Mende due to this cultural norm. The Mende do not tolerate such behavior from anyone, regardless of their status.

A young man who cannot control his sexual behavior in the township should focus his interest on a mature girl, lady, or widow through his host and formally propose marriage according to Mende traditions. On the wedding day, the groom must dance before the whole village, following the drumbeat and "shegureh," in front of his mother-in-law, which requires preparation if he does not know the dance.

Once married, life becomes easier for a stranger. Many people from various parts of the country who marry Mende women live peacefully among the Mende. The Mende are dignified and considerate toward strangers, who must observe this attitude when living among them. For example, one must wash hands properly before eating together, even if hungry, or they may be asked to wait for leftovers. This continues until the stranger demonstrates understanding of Mende customs, after which full inclusion is granted, giving a sense of belonging and confidence.

One important aspect of the Mende regarding marriage is investigating the background of the man proposing to their daughters before parents consent. This protects daughters from unknowingly entering into harmful relationships. If one does not have a suitable background, they should comply with these demands for safety. Marrying a Mende girl is generally not difficult for other tribes, but the rules are consequential.

Mothers carefully assess if the suitor genuinely loves their daughter, rather than simply being interested in her wealth or status. Questions asked include what will happen if the man runs out of money or finds a prettier and richer girl.

Regarding children and family life in the Mende community: Parents carry the responsibility of raising children to become successful and good citizens. The Mende take discipline seriously and provide full support to ensure children obtain sound educational qualifications before starting families. Education is seen as essential for life advancement.

The Mende believe it is their divine duty to ensure children receive quality education. The reward parents seek in return is respect from their children, which they value more than material gifts or food. Respect is considered the "pull-power" of success; a child lacking respect has no place in the family. Children who do not respect their parents, especially their fathers, are seen as strangers despite biological ties.

If a child shows persistent disrespect by age 18, fathers may lose hope and even question paternity. Such disrespect leads to lack of blessings and life difficulties, reflecting God's commandment to honor parents as stated in Exodus 20:1–21 and Deuteronomy 5:1–23. Politicians often show respect to the Mende because winning their goodwill influences political outcomes.

Young children are vulnerable to bad behavior influenced by peer pressure. Parents, especially fathers, respond firmly with discipline, including corporal punishment, in line with Proverbs 22:6 from the Holy Bible.

In the Mende community, raising a child is not the sole responsibility of the parents but the entire community. A child's safety is a community concern, and a child must respect everyone, addressing adults with proper titles. Calling adults by their first names is deemed disrespectful; titles based on age or status are used instead.

Disrespectful children are disliked and lack community favor. Those who show respect receive gifts, sympathy, and love. The cultural theory of respect applies to parents, too. Parental respect is crucial and enforced by discipline; disrespect invites harsh penalties, including beatings, which Sierra Leonean law permits.

If disrespect continues, parents may sever ties with such children. This causes the child to carry a "swear" (curse) that brings misfortune requiring traditional ceremonies and costly blessings to break.

Children with curses face ongoing hardships like barrenness and sickness, while respectful children enjoy endless blessings even after their parents have passed. Honoring parents aligns with biblical teachings (Exodus 20:12) and is both a cultural and divine mandate.

Parents do not expect payment for raising children but value respect as a sign of hope and determination to support their children through education. Daily prayers are encouraged to foster a relationship with God and invoke parental blessings. Mende children particularly fear their fathers, who provide for their educational and future needs. Early marriage is discouraged during schooling. When a boy marries, it is celebrated as a joy to God and the fulfillment of manhood and family establishment under God's authority to "be fruitful and multiply."

If children continue to disrespect their parents into adulthood, friendship and blessings with their fathers are lost, risking lifelong difficulties.

Regarding gay marriages:

Homosexual marriages are not recognized in Sierra Leone or much of Africa because such relationships are considered abnormal. Africans await divine guidance despite Western political pressures. Accepting same-sex relationships contradicts God's design because these unions cannot produce children.

Sexual relations between men or between women are seen as unnatural, as procreation is only possible through a man and woman. The Almighty God commands humans to "be fruitful and multiply" (Genesis 1:28), which is the foundational purpose of marriage.

Mende women rarely propose marriage to men, as doing so could damage their respectability. Women who do propose are often viewed as seeking sex or using men for material gain, while most men desire lifelong family settlements.

Some women break tradition motivated by the prospect of marrying successful men. Men are advised to safeguard their wealth carefully and to seek blessings from their mothers, which are believed to bring lasting success until they find the right partner.

Sierra Leone's increasing diversity has seen infiltration of foreign cultures, especially diamond-seekers and their families. Many women now break traditional barriers by proposing marriage on first meeting men.

CULTURAL DIFFERENCES-MY MENDE CULTURE:

The culture of the Mende, to which I belong, strongly emphasizes observing the seniority of people at all times, especially women who are older than you, typically within your mother's age group. The first sign of respect you give to such a woman is to keep your hands out of your pockets while slightly bowing with respect and honor. All such women are respectfully called "Yea", meaning mother, accompanied by a kind smile. If the woman is actually your mother—"Yea"—be prepared to give her a big hug. A man who has started working and earning money must always be ready to look after his mother first. It is customary to give your first salary entirely to your parents—your father and mother—and inform them that you have started working.

Upon receiving this money, they will give heartfelt blessings from the Almighty God and pray for your success at work. The father prays first, followed by the mother, who sits you on her lap and reminisces about your babyhood with affectionate jokes. Her prayers especially ask God to always be with you and to provide for you so you can continue to provide for her. She concludes with a blessing, "May God continue to bless you, Amen!" Afterward, when you want some cash for yourself, they may offer some, and when you leave, their parental blessings will flourish in your life wherever you go.

No joke: our mothers' blessings are very powerful in a young man's life, especially before marriage. Prioritizing girlfriends and spending money on them first does not reflect well on your character; it shows wastefulness. You will

realize this truth when you find your girlfriend with another man or when she leaves you because you cannot afford luxury possessions like a flashy car for summer outings.
This is the kind of protective magic that keeps us progressing in the UK without hindrance. Where did I learn this? From my Mende culture in Sierra Leone, from Bongor in the Koya Chiefdom of Kenema District, where my "Yea" gave birth to me. Do you like my culture?

ARE YOU INTERESTED IN GETTING MARRIED TO HAVE CHILDREN?

In Sierra Leone, both boys and girls are traditionally required to marry before having children, especially among the Mende people. The maturity age is not less than eighteen for girls and twenty for boys before beginning sexual relations. Couples must be mature enough to care for each other as husband and wife. The husband is generally older than the wife, though the age gap should not exceed ten years. Men are expected to marry when financially able to support their wife and future children.
Marriage is the first serious romantic commitment a man can offer a woman before she considers a relationship sincerely. Girls avoid casual "cross-leg over" relationships with men who are only interested in sex.

HOW DOES A MAN WIN OVER A YOUNG WOMAN TO START A RELATIONSHIP?

The process of establishing first contact and building trust is a subtle art. People come from different places and may meet by:
Seeing each other in the neighborhood
Meeting at school, college, or university
Meeting at work

Meeting on public transport
Meeting over the internet
Visiting each other's homes
Through personal introductions or matchmaking ("arranged contacting" that can lead to marriage)

The key is to build trust from the first meeting through light conversation or jokes to make the girl smile or remember something familiar. A man should ask permission before sharing something important, waiting patiently for her response. Eye contact is important but should not be too intense initially, as continuous direct staring may be seen as trying to control her.

If she responds positively, you may suggest meeting again for a meal or cinema. If encouraged, this is not a guarantee of obtaining her, but she is still open. The woman may reveal whether she is engaged or interested in marriage after careful consideration. Getting a serious Mende woman is not rushed.

During marriage proceedings, couples commonly ask each other, "Do you like this man to be your husband?" with mutual eye contact. The Mende believe that at this vow, holy angels unite the couple's souls before God for a lifelong union. They do not exchange rings but remain married forever spiritually.

My wife Sao and I took the same traditional vows in 1987 at her father's parlour in Konabu, near Kenema, Eastern Province of Sierra Leone. Though life has had its ups and downs, we trust God to sustain us until death. Our four children see us as Mohamed and Sao but in their own worlds.

Most relationships begin casually, often after drinking and dancing at nightclubs. Such relationships usually lack seriousness and are attempts to ease emotional pain.

Children result biologically from such encounters, though the parents may not marry. Children born outside marriage are often stigmatized as "baster," meaning street children without known fathers. Their mothers often seek respectable men to legitimize the child and seek forgiveness from God.

Regarding inheritance and family law:

Legally in Sierra Leone, a man and woman married and cohabiting have rightful ownership and responsibilities over their children and property. Fathers are responsible for financial support, including feeding, clothing, and maintenance. Fathers leading "playboy" lifestyles with multiple women have the firstborn with greater inheritance rights if that child respects the father.

Mothers who divorce and live with other men are generally not entitled to former husband's inheritance or related children's rights. Marriage is considered lifelong, and divorce is traditionally not accepted, consistent with Biblical principles.

Polygamy (one man with multiple wives) is not accepted by God, nor is a woman having multiple husbands ("monogamy" as described in the text). Couples should carefully commit to marriage as a lifelong journey without return.

A man may remarry only after his wife dies, and the woman must follow the same principle.

POLITICIANS GENERAL BEHAVIOUR WHEN IT COMES TO EDUCATION:

As Education is a lifelong mission of knowledge-seeking that begins in childhood and continues until grandparenthood. Educationists design and determine the contents of learning packages known as Education Curricula. Other educationists then deliver these designed contents to recipients at educational institutions called schools, which are divided into Nursery Schools (under 5s), Primary Schools, and Secondary Schools.

The “External Examining Bodies” are responsible for designing the contents of these education packages. They also draw and mark external examinations for subjects such as English Language, Mathematics, Geography, and Business Studies. Therefore, decisions about examination contents should come from these institutions, not politicians, who may lack the expertise regarding education content and its long-term societal impacts. Recently, UK politicians decided to offer "generosity" by reducing GCSE and A-Level course contents due to the Covid-19 pandemic. This, however, risks compromising the quality of education and future competitiveness of UK children in job markets.

This political move seems to be more about political correctness to gain popularity rather than genuinely considering the future impacts on children and society. Politicians should recognize that today's schoolchildren are future leaders whose education prepares them for the challenges of coming centuries. Education cannot be politicized; professional Examining Bodies should manage examinations and curriculum adjustments in response to crises like Covid-19.

Suggestions for British politicians include:

Cancelling exams temporarily and extending preparation time by a full year so children can cover the full curriculum without pressure.

Leaving examination content decisions to professional Examining Bodies rather than politicians.

Assessing the potential long-term learning gaps ("sinkholes") created by reduced curricula.

Education serves as the foundational taproot for Britain's development and should not be subject to hasty political interference. Historical examples, like Hazel Hill's mathematical contributions during WWII, remind us of the critical importance of solid education foundations.

In Sierra Leone, education reforms focus heavily on Primary and Secondary Schools. During his first state opening of Parliament on 10 May 2018, Julius Maada Bio officially launched Free Education in all primary and secondary schools. This development follows earlier measures under President Ahmad Tejan Kabbah, who had previously made WAEC (West African Secondary School Certificate) examinations free for all secondary school children, facilitating access to education in the post-civil war period.

These initiatives aim to widen access to education, recognizing its vital role in creating skilled future generations who will contribute to Sierra Leone's growth and stability.

APC Rule of Government in Sierra Leone	Rulers of APC in Sierra Leone	From	To
Prime Minister	Siaka Stevens	1967	1971 (4yrs)
President	Siaka Stevens	1971	1985(14yrs)
President	Joseph Saidu Momoh	1985	1992(7yrs)
President	Ernest Bai Koroma	2007	2018(11yrs)

TOTAL Number of APC mismanagements in Sierra Leone = 36 Years

President Bio's news for free education arrived with a sigh of relief and appreciation for many people in Sierra Leone, especially for large families with a number of children, which is just typical in many families where polygamy is practiced. This is practically normal for most Sierra Leonean families and this initiative came at the time when the defeated government of the APC has previously been responsible for the destruction of education psychologically without understanding the effects of their political greed on the country they claim to govern:

2018: LAUNCING FREE QUALITY EDUCATION"

In the academic year that started in September 2018, a "FREE QUALITY EDUCATION" was launched in Sierra

That education was a privilege for all those who can afford and that it was not meant to be free for all in Sierra Leone. The level of educational achievement in Sierra Leone, either primary, secondary, vocational college or university was not meant to be free but to pay for by those who feel it was beneficial for them. They claimed that education was just like any other product in a shop and that those who want to have, can have the product as long as they can afford the purchasing power. If you cannot afford, then you are left with your whish.
President Ernest Bai Koroma said that if children experiences poverty in their families that prevent them from getting or completing secondary school education and they do not have scholarships to complete their education, it was not the responsibility of the government to pay for their education.
However, that was one of the legacies of Siaka Stevens who founded the APC political party in Sierra Leone in 1960 and that was why he did not encourage education in his birth place, the Northern Province. Has quite aware of the benefits of education but he was just too scared and greedy that if people of the North were to become educated, they will stand for political chances against him.

What is the state of condition for the arrival of this "Free Quality Education" in Sierra Leone? If we are to be honest with ourselves, the state of condition here is that the arrival of this system his given birth to many unexpected scenarios. Some are viewing it as a political ploy to for the SLPP to gain victory over the APC. Some are also viewing it as a "shocking-bite" that took education seekers by surprise and as a means of wooing the voters for the SLPP's future votes. No matter how much criticism the opposition parties level against this new initiative, the positive virtues cannot be dismissed or overlooked for political reasons. Political systems come and go, always leaving behind both good and bad legacies. If the Free Quality Education system is maintained and properly directed, I believe the legacy left by President Maada Bio's government will benefit the future of everyone in this country.

However, I have some concerns about the Free Education recently launched by President Maada Bio. Politicians in Africa often sing the tunes that people want to hear to gain applause, so I wonder if this Free Education initiative was partly a political campaign strategy to garner popularity and applause from the people.

Nevertheless, beyond political motives, the Free Quality Education program has become a significant step in Sierra Leone since its launch in 2018. It aims to provide tuition-free education from primary through secondary levels, including free teaching materials and examination fee coverage. The program has expanded educational access to millions of children, particularly benefiting those from disadvantaged backgrounds. While political motivations may exist, the tangible benefits of this initiative for national development and future generations are increasingly evident if sustained and managed well.

> The stakeholders of education in Sierra Leone are: Adequate school buildings, school children, parents/guardians of school children, school teachers, school auxiliary staffs, school learning materials, transportation to schools, school lunch provisions and school uniforms; School examination bodies (WAEC), School inspectors, employers of school leavers, Post-secondary educational institutions (Universities and vocational training colleges) the Ministry of Education Parents of school children, Villages of Sierra Leone, Animals of Sierra Leone, Plants of Sierra Leone, Fishes in the rivers of Sierra Leone, Earthworms in the soil of Sierra Leone and the President of Sierra Leone, (who at the time of writing this book is: President Julius Maada Bio).

It is still very common to see children who are supposed to be in school at specific times, engaged in either street petty trading or playing in different corners of their communities and yet still, we are talking about free education in the country in Sierra Leone.

> *Your concerns about the Free Quality Education (FQE) program in Sierra Leone are well-founded and reflect challenges documented in various reports. Accountability issues arise when documentation is incomplete or inaccurate, such as when school registers contain names of students who do not attend regularly ("ghost students"). This leads to government funds being misused, often without sufficient oversight. Schools may claim resources for children not effectively participating in school, causing waste and potential corruption.*
>
> *Effective free education systems require robust monitoring and control mechanisms. Sierra Leone's Ministry of Basic and Senior Secondary Education (MBSSE) conducts annual school censuses and deploys District Education Officers for supervision, but capacity gaps and infrastructural deficits limit their efficiency. Problems like teacher shortages, overcrowded classrooms, and poor data management compound the difficulty in enforcing strict controls on attendance and resource allocation.*
>
> *Regarding school feeding, providing daily free meals in primary schools is crucial for motivation and*

attendance, especially for children from poverty-affected families. Hunger is a major barrier to learning. Although some feeding programs exist, their coverage remains inconsistent and often event-driven (e.g., "independent day" or Christmas), rather than daily and nationwide, reducing their overall impact.

Political leadership responsibility is vital to enforce policies and maintain system integrity. While President Julius Maada Bio's government has made significant strides in education reform, practical challenges persist, including the effective involvement of skilled professionals in managing the FQE. Concerns about political interference and mismanagement emphasize the need for transparent governance models, separating political influence from administrative control.

In comparison, countries like England maintain tight governmental oversight of school enrollment, attendance, and absentee follow-up, often in collaboration with parents and communities. Sierra Leone could benefit from adapting elements of such models to strengthen its own free education system.

Lastly, politics and leadership in Africa face broader systemic challenges. Leaders are ideally born with inherent skills and a divine call to serve, but politicians—elected by people—often face criticisms of corruption and neglect. Strong democratic accountability mechanisms are needed to ensure that political leadership translates into genuine public service, including effective education provision.

Thus, tackling the FQE challenges demands governmental commitment to transparency, professional management, data integrity, resource allocation, and community engagement to ensure education benefits all children equitably.

PREGNANT SCHOOL GIRLS IN SIERRA LEONE:

I came across in the internet news that Sierra Leone has ordered to revoke ban on pregnant schoolgirls, meaning that schoolgirls who become pregnant are allowed in schools to continue with their schooling up till the time they give birth to the children they carry in their stomachs.

Pregnant schoolgirls no longer banned from school in Sierra Leone

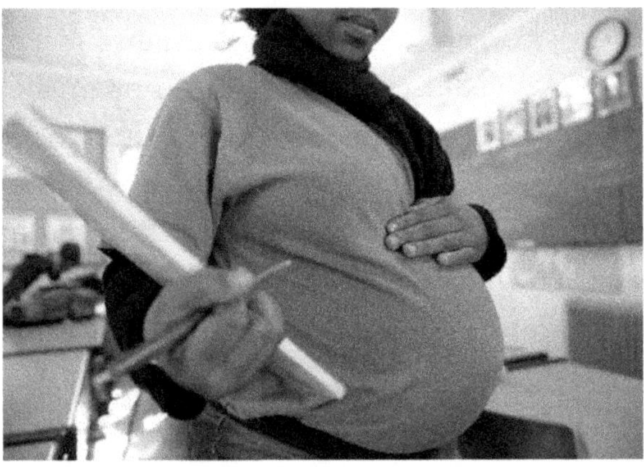

The caption on news headline, *"Sierra Leone ordered to revoke ban on pregnant schoolgirls"* of (Fri 13 Dec 2019 09.00 GMT) published in the Guardian Newspaper, came as a shocking news and especially when the publication further went on saying that *'a regional court ordered the immediate overturn of a "discriminatory" policy that has denied tens of thousands the right to finish their education'.* I think the government of Sierra Leone has got this ruling wrong, especially on humanity grounds. Remember that the United Nation has ruled that every human being has the right to be protected and prevented from death by their governments.

Therefore, this regional court ruling is not considering human protection relating to the pregnant school girls who are allowed to continue schooling. They are human

beings and their protection should be of paramount to the head of state in the country.
Has President Julius Maada Bio considered this fact or is he putting the priority of the so-called Regional Court in Nigeria with different sovereignty over the human population (School girls) in Sierra Leone, so that when another wave of civil war break out is Sierra Leone, the Nigeria government will send over their military to redeem Sierra Leone as they did when President Ahmad Tejan Kabbah was in power? Is this what President Bio is letting us to understand and believe?

Political correctness often arises when politicians seek to avoid alienating voters whose support is crucial for election victories, even if some societal views find certain issues controversial. For example, acceptance of gays (homosexuals and lesbians) in many developed countries is viewed by some as disobedient to God and aligned with negative forces. There is a concern that Sierra Leone might inadvertently take a similar direction due to political correctness. It seems President Bio may have adopted a politically cautious stance regarding LGBTQ issues, influenced by regional bodies like ECOWAS during the Sierra Leone civil war, prioritizing political stability over addressing the psychological impacts on young Sierra Leoneans—a common instinct among African leaders.
In some countries, there are even campaigns to legalize bestiality (marriage between humans and animals like dogs), and certain families criminalize no sexual conduct within incestuous relationships, such as intercourse with a wife's sister, daughters, biological siblings, or a father's young wives. Let me categorically

[In Sierra Leone, male same-sex sexual activity remains illegal and can carry life imprisonment, though enforcement is rare. Female same-sex activity is legal. The constitution does not protect against discrimination based on sexual orientation, and same-sex marriage is not recognized. Anti-discrimination laws in employment based on sexual orientation were introduced in 2023 but are limited in scope. The government has resisted broader LGBTQ rights reforms, balancing international pressure with local cultural and religious norms.]
say at this point that those who are or have engaged in such behaviours have already taken into the wrong directions as stated in the following verses of the Holy Bible: Corinthians 5:1, 18:6-7, 18:8-10, 18, 18:11-17, Deuteronomy 27:20 .... Check them out and perhaps they can later on find out how to cry to the Almighty God and to show them how to repent; how to refrain from sinful activities of such which are forbidden. These forbidden sexual orgies "with animals" are constantly going on in almost many cities in most developed countries, in the description of modern civilization and liberal democratic values. Therefore, considering the political correctness of this Regional Court ruling I think, has set the landmark for pregnant school girls into more trouble and less consideration for their humanity.

Is the SLPP government considering modern development to come to this type of modern value in our Sierra Leone? The ruling has erased the line between what is good and moral behaviour and what is not good and is considered as immoral behaviours. If children are developing in a learning society with no recognition of knowing their boundaries, what will their future output become? Do we expect our children to be educated without knowing ethical mannerisms and what they are required to refrain from? Are we ready to sacrifice our children for the political victory of politicians so that they can stay in power? If I am to ask, "What benefits will the country get out of this kind of court ruling?" To motivate the girls or dehumanise them? When women become pregnant with their first babies, the care for them becomes very paramount because at that time, they need special attention including the babies in their stomachs. Is the government considering this?

Allowing pregnant schoolgirls to continue attending school invites potential punishment and suffering due to pregnancy during schooling. To some extent, I do not entirely blame these girls because the forces of nature take their course when genetics are connected. These girls become pregnant only when they have sexual intercourse with men. What consequences exist for the men responsible for impregnating these girls? Are they assuming they can enjoy themselves and escape accountability by throwing Le5,000.00 notes at the girls? I believe such irresponsible behavior cannot be tolerated in this country, and President Maada Bio must not allow it—even if it involves members of his cabinet. If no one else will say it, then I am categorically stating it now! Pregnant schoolgirls should not be allowed to continue attending school until six months after delivery, allowing for proper post-natal leave.

Post-Natal Holiday *is designed to help new mothers recover from* ***pregnancy*** *and* **childbirth**, *while they spend time with their new baby. Under our expert guidance, we'll help them safely repair their body and restore their strength. This is the human right of all new mothers of human beings including our children (school girls who become pregnant in Sierra Leone). The basic human rights of girls who become pregnant cannot be violated and the regional court in Nigeria should understand this and should not take bullish tactics on our girls in Sierra Leone.*

If the government accepts that schoolgirls will become pregnant in Sierra Leone, it must provide all necessary facilities to make life comfortable for them and their children, both before and after birth. What some courts may forget is that no female can become pregnant without sexual contact with a male. Only God performed the miraculous conception when the Holy Spirit caused the virgin Mary to conceive Jesus (Luke 1:26–38). Mary was not allowed to attend school while pregnant, and I make no apology for stating this as a faithful Christian.

Allowing pregnant girls in schools exposes them to danger and undermines the educational environment, which is meant for children focusing on developing their futures. Educational psychologists at Buckingham University emphasize that learning environments must be suitable for cognitive, behavioral, and developmental factors impacting education outcomes.

Political correctness, by allowing pregnant schoolgirls to attend school, abuses both the learning environment and the rights of all students. It is a violation of their human rights in broad daylight. Schoolgirls are underage and should not become pregnant. They become so through sexual intercourse, which is wrong when involving underage girls. Local courts should require the girls to name the males involved, and then the law must severely punish these men for engaging sexually with schoolgirls.

Girls must be controlled, not left free to engage in sexual activities casually. Men must also limit their sexual exploits and avoid schoolgirls, allowing the girls to pursue education until maturity. This is essential for a decent society where all behave respectfully. Let us engage in sex with decency, both male and female.

AREA OF CAUTION:

Since independence in 1961, Sierra Leone's opposition party, the All Peoples Congress (APC), founded by Siaka Stevens in 1960, has ruled for 36 years—longer than the SLPP, founded in 1951. Why then has the country's educational system, once a leader in Africa, deteriorated to a substandard level today?

Have the politicians forgotten to take on board that the development of a country can only be possible through the development of education in that country?

When the late President Robert Mugabe rule over Zimbabwe since ***1980 with the Zimbabwean African Nationalist Party –Patriotic Front (ZANU-PF) until 2017*** *when he was placed under house arrest until his resignation that year, the Zimbabweans still appreciate his long ruling of this country because he was able to leave a long lasting legacy with them and which nobody will ever take away. That legacy is* ***EDUCATION.***

Robert Mugabe's first wife was Sally Mugabe. They got married in 1987 but she died in 1992 and thereafter, Robert Gabriel Mugabe remarried another wife, Grace Ntombzodwa Mugabe a South African, who remained as the First Lady of Zimbabwe until when he resigned in 2017.

What propelled the military action that placed President Robert Mugabe under house arrest in 2017 was due to the tension that climaxed around the political situation in the country; which emerged from the First Lady. She was discovered to have been considering to persuade Robert Mugabe to leave her in charge of the country as a president, to transfer ownership of the presidency of the state to her as his successor wife, should anything happens to the president, that she would remain in control as the president of Zimbabwe. She came up with this fantasy, especially when Mr. Mugabe was now an old man.

She became just out of control and got power thirsty. She engaged into ***"I don't care"*** *shouting with strong fists of the air on the Zimbabwean political platform with President Mugabe.*

She further engaged into land grabbing and claiming ownership unreasonably to a great tension that Coup d'état started smelling in the ear.

The military leader at that time was Major General Sibusiso Busi Moyo who used his initiative, and as a cleverly educated Zimbabwean, to put the president under house arrest to protect the safety of his life.

Major General Sibusiso Busi Moyo *is now retired from the military and serving Zimbabwe, the country he so preciously love, as a politician and in the capacity of Minister of Foreign Affairs and International Trade in the Cabinet of President Emmerson Mnangagwa of Zimbabwe since November 2017. Such a tactful fighter is the type of leaders, we need in positions to rule African countries.*

Zimbabwean lesson has become a typical case study, to learn from and to beware of African leaders' newly married wives, such as our First-Lady in Sierra Leone. There is no malice attached here to the fact of the politics of our country. When anything happens in any part of the world, we always add to our learning experience in order to enrich our intelligence and brain packages. ***This Zimbabwean experience is a very good one to learn from and to understand that when the Almighty God is ready to solve problems of his created human beings, he will step in at uninvited and unexpected time.***

Have the All Peoples Congress (APC) politicians in this country, ever been focused on the development of education here for the benefits of the human generations after their ruling? What is their proof and evidence?

Is this not a clear indication that if a political party rules over a country for a considerable period of time, it may result into ruining very important fabrics of the society of that country that may be difficult to rectify and put in place when the party goes out of office?

Is this not an indication that the APC political party in Sierra Leone had ruined a series of the fabrics of our country (particularly, the education sector) and this happened only because of the long duration of that political party rules for "thirty six" (36) years in power, mismanaging the country's human resources.

REMINDING THE VOTERS ABOUT PRESIDENT JULIUS MAADA BIO's PROMISES ON 12 MAY 2018.

Here again, the voters in Sierra Leone are reminded about the promise of President Julius Maada Bio on the state opening of parliament in his inaugural speech on 12 May 2018 that he made on Education in Sierra Leone. To what extent have these promise been fulfilled or fulfilling. Are conditions in Sierra Leone about basic education still the same in Sierra Leone before that statement? If changes are taking place in this direction, how are these changes effecting in provincial village schools that are involved in delivering basic education in Sierra Leone?

Improving Education and Skills Training

52. The primary objective of the New Direction is to increase access to quality pre-primary, primary, secondary, technical and vocational education and training as well as university education that will enable them engage in meaningful productive economic activity. To demonstrate our commitment to education, my Government will increase and sustain budgetary allocation to education to a minimum of 20% of the national budget.

53. The change in the education system from **6-3-3-4 to 6-3-4-4** is challenging. The existing classroom blocks and teachers are not adequate to meet the needs of pupils for an additional year of schooling. This change in the educational system has also impacted on teenage pregnancy and early school leaving among girls who consider the number of years of schooling to be too many. There is no evidence to show that it has improved learning outcomes. Rather, it has imposed pressure on Government for additional classrooms and promoted teenage pregnancy. In fulfilment of my Manifesto commitment, we shall revert to the **6-3-3-4** system of education. The relevant authorities will advise when it will be best for this change to be effective. To improve on the system, My Government intends to increase contact hours, build additional classrooms, eliminate the two shift system and develop technical and vocational education.

54. Mr. Speaker, Honourable Members, I am pleased to officially pronounce that effective next academic year starting September 2018, my Government will introduce Free Education from primary level to senior secondary school as promised. I have already engaged many of our partners for support of this programme and I am pleased to report that, our international and donor partners have expressed commitments to support my administration. To ensure effective coordination of support of this programme, Government will establish a Multi-Partner Education for Development Basket Fund. In support of this, two Committees will be established. First, a High Level Inter-Ministerial and Partners Group (IMPG) on Free Education comprising of relevant ministries and partners will be set up. This Group will provide the strategic guidance to the planning and design of the programme, mobilise resources and oversee the implementation. Second, a Technical Group (TG) on Education comprising professionals from the relevant MDAs and partner agencies will be established to design the programme, coordinate and monitor the implementation. The Technical Group will report to the High Level Inter Ministerial and Partners Group.

55. Mr. Speaker, Honourable Members, improving education governance is critical for the success of the New Direction in education. To this end, my Government will (i) review the Education Sector Plan to ensure it is realigned with the priorities of the New Direction (ii) strengthen Education Management and Information System (EMIS) to support informed strategic decision-making (iii) develop a robust policy and legal framework for Public-Private-Partnership in the education sector (iv) develop the capacity of School Inspectorate for effective school monitoring and supervision (v) build the capacity of School Management Committees (SMC) (vi) de-politicise the Board of Governors of schools, redefine their roles, and introduce a compulsory reporting requirement (vii) respect and support the autonomy of the National Union of Students (NUSS) and (viii) promote social dialogue with relevant stakeholders in the education service delivery including the Sierra Leone Teachers Union.

56. Mr. Speaker, Honourable Members, none of us would have been here today without our greatest asset, teachers. Yet, they have been least recognized and least rewarded. This is demotivating. Let me simply state that without qualified teachers, our Free Education Programme will not be fully implemented. In the New Direction, Government will raise the morale and productivity of our teachers. To this end, I hereby pronounce a Presidential Initiative for Teachers. The Initiative will ensure that matters relating to teachers are treated with utmost importance. Additionally, my administration will (i) review and make functional the Teaching Service Commission (ii) develop a special incentive scheme for Science and French teachers as well as teachers in remote areas and those in special needs institutions (iii) introduce.

THE BEST TEACHER Award Scheme for the most innovative, ingenious and dedicated teachers at national and district levels (iv) provide free university education for three children of every school teacher with at least 10 years' teaching experience.

57. There is limited number of qualified teachers at all levels. Only 55 percent of teachers at pre-school level, 42 percent at primary level, 35 percent at Junior Secondary School, 49% at Senior Secondary School, are qualified to teach. Increasing the number of qualified teachers and ensuring fair distribution amongst districts is critical for the successful implementation of our Free Education Programme. In support of this, my administration will establish Teacher Training campuses in all districts, expand and improve on distance learning education for teachers and provide free tuition for teacher education.

58. Mr. Speaker, Honourable Members, the amounts of public spending on fee subsidy for university education is unsustainable. Whilst we will improve on the management of the Grants-in-Aid policy, my administration will introduce Students Loan Scheme that will provide loans to deserving students to access higher education.

59. Mr. Speaker, Free Education will increase demand for school. As a progressive Government, we need to prepare for the anticipated increase in school enrolment. Therefore, my administration will adopt a policy of One-Administrative Section-One Primary School, One-Electoral Ward-One Junior Secondary School and One-Electoral Constituency-One-Senior Secondary School. Additionally, my Government will construct new classroom blocks in urban towns to reduce congestion in schools and eventually eliminate the two-shift system in the next few years.

60. To sustain high school enrolment and improve learning, my administration will work with World Food Programme and other food agencies as well as the Ministry of Agriculture and Forestry to expand school feeding programmes in all public assisted primary schools.

61. The cost of transportation constitutes a major share of urban household expenditure on education. This high cost of urban transportation causes lateness and affect school attendance which further affect learning. My Government will re-introduce school bus system in large urban towns on a cost recovery basis and less than the prevailing market price.

62. Mr. Speaker, Honourable Members, the high level of adult illiteracy in Sierra Leone estimated at 60 percent is unacceptable in any progressive nation. As part of my commitment to education, my administration will work with partners to develop and implement cost effective strategies for providing basic literacy and numeracy training for our adults who were not fortunate to attend school. Some of these will include (i) initially establishing one functional adult literacy centre in every district and later expanding to every chiefdom using existing school facilities and (ii) integrating literacy programmes into agricultural and livelihood programmes.

63. The New Direction believes that training is the foundation for enhancing the country's competitiveness. To this end, my Government will (i) review and standardise the curriculum and certification for Technical and Vocational Education and Training (TVET) (ii) develop a national apprenticeship scheme which can provide internship for trainees of TVET institutes and at the same time provide direct training for youth and (iii) develop a robust Public-Private-Partnership framework to increase private sector participation in TVET training. Also, my Government will establish in every district capital one Polytechnic Institution that will be fully equipped with modern tools and equipment for technical vocational education and training in areas with high potential for job creation among the population.

As education is about the development of community human development so that the people living in that community will

64. Mr. Speaker, the conditions of our institutions of higher learning and in particular the citadel of knowledge, University of Sierra Leone and Njala University are deplorable. We have lost the glory of being the Athens of West Africa. We require urgent actions to develop our Universities and all other higher institutions. Already, my Government has created a separate Ministry of Technical and Higher Education that will solely focus on technical and higher education. My intention is to establish a university system that employs its own leadership as chancellors and Vice Chancellors with distinguished and proven records of higher education leadership and significant international clout and contacts (funding and research networks). In this light, effective 2019, I as President will cease to be the Chancellor of the University of Sierra Leone. In the coming months, the 2005 Universities Act will be reviewed to reflect this and many other changes where necessary.

65. Science and Technology is the bedrock for the development of any modern economy. Unfortunately, in Sierra Leone, the schools and colleges lack even the basic facilities for scientific research. My Government is setting up a Directorate for Science, Technology and Innovation to develop a framework for scientific research. Initially, this Directorate will be midwifed in the Office of the President but shall work closely with the Ministry of Technical and Higher Education. 17 66. Mr. Speaker, Honourable Members, one of the reasons for attitudinal challenges is limited civic education.

This is compounded by mass illiteracy among the population. If we are to develop as a nation, we must educate our people on rights, responsibilities and obligations as good citizens. To this end, my Government will launch a National Civic Education Programme to provide civic education in our educational institutions and communities. Additionally, my administration will direct that civics be re-introduced in our schools and colleges, comprehensive curriculum for all levels will be developed and civic educators be provided training to cascade the training in schools.

learn to know what they can do with utilisation of their natural human resources, the need for education in Sierra Leone cannot be over looked.

"Education is the process of searching to known, what you do not know; until you know. Therefore, it is always an investigation into the unknown".

The arrival of educational progress does not come quickly but requires time, patience, and dedication. Therefore, I see no reason why parents and the public cannot wait gradually to witness future harvests from current efforts.

If President Julius Maada Bio had not taken education seriously in his first term and delayed until the later stages of his leadership to focus on education, he would have risked losing the presidency. He was clever enough to keep education as a key priority throughout his political campaigns.

Are all schools in Sierra Leone supplied with free school meals daily to ensure children are fed and able to concentrate on learning? Are quality facilities such as clean drinking water consistently available in these schools?

Given that President Julius Maada Bio's SLPP government has introduced and launched Free Quality Education nationwide, does it truly cover all children in every school across the country? Are village schools in rural provinces receiving similar services and resources as those in cities and provincial headquarters? Village schools should not be left behind, as there are many talented students there needing support.

HANDS-OFF-OUR-GIRLS:

Mrs. Fatima Bio, wife of President Julius Maada Bio, is a woman known for her public initiatives that bring attention to the administration. She is titled the “First Lady” and launched the “HANDS-OFF OUR GIRLS” project in Freetown, gaining attention among Sierra Leoneans in the US and UK diaspora through fundraising activities.

Although Mrs. Fatima Bio professes love for her husband, she is not the president and has limited influence on the political platform of Sierra Leone. Their marital relationship should remain private and not become a political platform, as she lacks the skills to engage in politics. She claims to support the SLPP but is not registered as a party member. She may have unintentionally overstepped by engaging politically without proper discussion or support, capitalizing on her status as First Lady.

Her father is Gambian, and her mother is Sierra Leonean. Has Mrs. Bio consulted the Sierra Leone National Constitution regarding political involvement given her mixed heritage? Her political activities have caused discomfort among genuine politicians and registered SLPP voters. It is essential for her to confine her role to family matters, as her political involvement is neither appropriate nor beneficial to the party.

She once referred to Sierra Leoneans with PhDs as “the most stupid educated people” politically, claiming they “shoot themselves in the foot” when speaking. If this is her view, why does President Maada Bio continue to surround himself with educated professionals in his cabinet?

Is this kind of statements not back-biting our president's efforts for the developments and other areas of our needs in this country? Serious and ambitious people work hard and tirelessly to get themselves educated to the level of PhD and they do not tolerate that kind of silly comments from anyone who belittles them on SLPP political platforms, especially in the diaspora of SLPPUK/I.

We have every right to believe that the First Lady's Psychological Behavioural spiel-over effects are building up into "negative effects" on membership build-ups for the SLPP, especially during the political campaigns. Continuation of her attitudes may lead to breaking- away, the SLPP into fabrics that she has no ability to put together. Is she working a "Negative Psychological Applications" whose effects can lead to negative reactions on SLPP for which nobody can hold her responsible for , under our eyes, including those of President Julius Maada Bio? Therefore, she must stop with her abusive approaches, both socially and religiously. Muslims and Christians have been living together for years, before her father arrived in our country from The Gambia, in search of diamonds. We are very special peaceful people and we want to remain as such. We don't want a Religious disunity that may be resulted into a segment that may be referred to as "Religious War" between Christians and Muslims in our country. She is not a politician and she has not yet been elected into office, as the President of Sierra Leone. She is just the wife of President Julius Maada Bio and NOT the "Deputy President".

President Julius Maada Bio is encouraged to have a private 'one-to-one' discussion with his wife, Mrs. Fatima Bio, to ensure she is fully aware of any political developments or maneuvering—especially within other political parties in Sierra Leone—that he may not know about but needs to be informed of. This conversation would be in the best interest of the Sierra Leone People's Party (SLPP), the party both are associated with.

Mrs. Fatima Bio has referred to President Maada Bio as the "King of Kings" during a fundraising event in America. It is important to clarify that this title is reserved for Jesus Christ alone. No one on earth should be called "The King of Kings," including President Maada Bio. From a Christian perspective, Jesus Christ is the Almighty God who came to Earth, loves humanity, and provides guidance on how people should live (as explained in John 14:6-14, Matthew 10:27-34, Luke 10:22). Mrs. Fatima Bio's religious upbringing in The Gambia might not have fully educated her on this, but there is opportunity for her to learn.

Calling President Maada Bio by this title risks igniting religious tensions between Christians and Muslims in Sierra Leone, which is a sensitive and potentially dangerous issue. Many Christians feel uncomfortable with her approach but may remain silent until election time, when their votes can express their dissatisfaction.

Mrs. Fatima Bio's social media comments—such as telling people who spread "fake news" about the president to "go sit in their toilets"—raise concerns about whether she understands the implications of such statements and their impact on her reputation as First Lady. Her involvement in political rhetoric, despite not being a registered politician, risks alienating SLPP supporters and disrupting party unity.

Sierra Leone's political history includes a decade-long civil war, partly fueled by divisive politics, so careful attention to rhetoric is crucial. The First Lady's political involvement should be limited, allowing President Maada Bio to focus on governance while she supports from the sidelines as expected of a presidential spouse.

It is also notable that Mrs. Fatima Bio's Gambian heritage has drawn attention; concerns have been raised regarding potential souring of relations between Sierra Leone and The Gambia. Sierra Leoneans respect their long-standing, positive relationship with The Gambia and expect continued harmony. Many children of Sierra Leonean-Gambian parentage live in The Gambia today, and they fall under Sierra Leone's constitution if involved in politics.

Lastly, there are rumors of Mrs. Fatima Bio's connections with influential individuals within the rival APC party, which could complicate her role within the SLPP. It is urged that she focus on her supportive duties as the president's wife and refrain from political ambitions that could detract from the party's cohesion and national leadership.

The "Hands-off Our Girls" campaign was launched as a key initiative to protect girls' education in Sierra Leone, particularly to combat early and forced marriages that have historically disrupted many girls' educational journeys. The campaign aims to criminalize the actions of men who sexually exploit schoolgirls rather than punishing the girls themselves.

Mrs Fatima Bio's father came to Sierra Leone in search of diamonds in Kono, and many Gambians are involved in similar "gold digging" trade. There he came across a young beautiful Sierra Leonean (Kono) lady and asked her hand for marriage. This was how Mrs. Fatima Bio was born to a Gambian father Mr. Umar Jabbie on 27 November 1980 by a Sierra Leonean lady, the year when our country hosted the Organisation of African Unity (OAU) at the Bintumani Hotel. That same year in 1980, was the first international political engagement of the late President Robert Mugabe of Zimbabwe. He will ever be remembered as one of the champions of education for Africans under the Zimbabwean African Nationalist Union Patriotic Front (ZANU-PF) in his country, where he defeated Canaan Banana, one of the ceremonial presidents of the then parliamentary republic.

Mr Robert Mugabe himself was a teacher by profession who saw that Apartheid was wrong for Zimbabwe and the rest of the Southern Africa region, which prompted him into arms conflicts, under Earn Smith.

In rural village settings, however, traditional cultural values shape family decisions differently. Many families do not send their girls to school but instead teach them farming or domestic skills. Marriage often occurs immediately upon reaching maturity to prevent societal conflict over marriage prospects, with the presentation of kolanut as a traditional marriage proposal to the girl's parents. Pregnancy before marriage is a serious source of shame for both the girl and her family. The child born out of wedlock is stigmatized as a "bastard" in these communities.

> Village girls typically approach marriage with great seriousness, respecting themselves and their families. A common saying is a girl will insist that a man "keep his private part in his trousers" until he

formally proposes marriage through her parents, reflecting respect for herself, her family, and her future children.

Since its launch in December 2018, spearheaded by First Lady Fatima Bio and supported by President Julius Maada Bio, the campaign has worked to raise awareness, influence policy, and support girls' access to reproductive health care and justice. It has led to improvements such as the introduction of a Fast-Track Special Court for rape cases, training of medical professionals, and distribution of sanitary pads to schoolgirls to reduce educational interruptions during menstruation.

The campaign seeks to empower girls and women to speak out against abuse, promoting their right to education and protection from early marriage and sexual violence. It mobilizes local leaders, including paramount chiefs and religious figures, to support its goals and foster societal change.

MATURITY OF A GIRL

What are the signs of maturity in a girl? When a girl develops a pair of breasts on her chest, she is kept clean with long hairs, shaky bottoms and clean teeth with beautiful laughing and big clean eyes, with two dimples on her cheek,she will begin to attract young men. These are the signs to invite her into association that may sometimes end up into invitation to have sex and sometimes, circumstances will find it difficult to resist and fall on the no ground.

Where these invitations are many, she may yield to one or even more and thereafter, develops the habits of enjoying the habits of being promiscuous. Eventually, girls of such habits may become pregnant with no specifically identified father of the child and all those men who have been sleeping with her will hide from her vicinity.

When such happens to a girl in a village, it becomes a very big scandal on her parents and members of her entire family. Therefore, parents are trying all out to avoid such happenings to their daughters and thus forcing them into earlier marriages whenever the signs begin to show. Maturity signs in girls vary in individuals; from girls-to-girls. Some girls start showing their maturities from the age of 16 and so on. Eighteen years old is the recommended age for human maturity but this is not an international case in all cultures such as ours in Sierra Leone. Since "Hands – Off Our Gils" was launched and funds raised internationally and in many areas of districts in Sierra Leone, we have seen nothing coming out of the

Project that is so far beneficial to the girls of Sierra Leone, which can be described as fighting for the right of girls. We have heard of a case in the social media, of a case relating to the abuse of a toddler girl, by her elder brother who got the young girl killed to avoid being exposed. Her mother ran away with a boyfriend, in the absence of the girl's father. So, what is happening, especially with the money being raised for "Hands-Off Our Girls" project?

All we heard was that what happened in the poor girl's death was a family issue and it has already been put to rest. We don't accept that kind of family ties in Sierra Leone and we demand that the girl's death is brought back to justice.

Therefore, in order for people in our rural villages in Sierra Leone to understand "Hand-Off our Girls" properly, it should have been launched and implemented through ***"Civic Education Methods"*** *in courageous manners that will let the people in our rural areas who never went to school; (and they do not know how to read and write), to understand and appreciate well, rather than delivering from* ***"My husband's political platform".*** *The people in my village do not understand the meaning of "First Lady". This method is a mockery of presenting what one does not understand".* ***Education must be delivered through methods of understanding which will make it meaningful.***

This kind of political behaviour is not one of our styles in Sierra Leone.

The "Hands-Off Our Girls" project was seen by many as being enveloped as a "welfare package" boosting all special education encouragements and motivation for particularly all girls' education in Sierra Leone. We clearly see that this package is quite different from our perception, and our expectations have developed some far extremes of fear in us after deeper analysis.

We have now come to realize that we have been easily switched off from thinking about our own past, thinking about how our traditional parents were teaching our girls in those days to look after their monthly periods and they controlled and restricted themselves in public and other places with devised monthly and reliable period pads. We had all rights to question and allow our girls the utilization of these "sanitary period-pads" made in factories outside this country without knowing the composition in its making.

Why have we forgotten to realize that the First Lady is just an ordinary human being like many of the women born and grew up in this country?

We put all our trust in her because she is the wife of the president of this country, and little did we put a check to find out first what she (Fatima Bio) was about to do in our country and what was or were her achievement targets for this country, our country Sierra Leone?

However, let me inform all Sierra Leoneans that it is not yet too late to rectify our mistakes to bring back into our right position to save our lovely Sierra Leone, hence the next general election in this country is 2028, and the time I am writing this information is 14 October 2025, which is over two years before we go into the general election.

All of Fatima Bio's activities have been:

targeting the poor people in Sierra Leone to rely upon her as a God-sent savior to take Sierra Leone out of what she describes as out of poverty.

Her project of "Hands-Off Our Girls" has been targeting school girls as a method of holding our children tighter in a way that when they get used to using sanitary period pads they will not want to go without them and that will be the time for her to dictate to them and their parents what she wants from them. To vote for her! Those who or their parent refuse to obey her will go without or will enter into prostitution to get money to buy the sanitary pads from pharmacies even when some of their poor parents cannot afford.

Fatima Bio has been disrupting most strategic SLPP political meetings and elections across the country to put her own supporters only to positions and sometimes, removing key role players at strategic places who are replaced by her own choices who have started turning up negatively producing because they are not the people's choices in their communities as has been happening in key strategic areas of SLPP in certain major cities; such as in Kenema, Kailahun, Pujehun and more other areas.

Fatima Bio has now clearly demonstrated that she is not definitely a supporter and member of the SLPP. She has been and she is still in favor of the APC. To verify this statement that it is not just an accusation, it shows clearly in her political instincts that propel her relationships with the APC giants of Sylvia Olayinka Blyden and Ivonne Aki-Sawyer.

For your information, my research discoveries have found out that Fatima has been a time bomb planted on the SLPP awaiting to explode when there is right. They think that Fatima has now matured in Sierra Leone politics enough to disrupt the SLPP's achievement so that they can transfer power back to APC. Fatima is working on this agenda hard to make it possible with Komba Kandeh Yumkella-KKY.

Fatima Jabbie-Bio is now frustratingly saying in her political campaign messages that even if she dies now, she will return on earth and will become SLPP. But this reincarnation she is talking about is never possible and has never happened in Sierra Leone. If she listened to any of her nonsense and flamboyant nonsense of that kind, you will be supporting her to shit on the clean pathway of the SLPP. We don't want anybody to die and come back to lead SLPP for us in this country. When she comes back from dead, it is better for her to go to The Gambia, perhaps they have a place for such dead people, but we have no such evil places in Sierra Leone for people returning from the dead. We don't do that kind of Gambian-JUJU in our country, let Fatima Bio not be encouraged to introduce juju practice in our country, Sierra Leone through marriage. We worship the Almighty God through the Holy Spirit, not Satan the evil spirit through Fatima Bio.

Fatima Jabbie-Bio is a money grabber even from the pockets of dying patients who have suffered from illness for the rest of their lives and she cares for nothing out of that.

There was a coup attempt that failed recently in Freetown in 2023 alleged to have been orchestrated by retired president Ernest Bai Koroma, when the country was "upside-down" and President Bio was quite busy at that time with the running of the state, trying to put our lives together. That was the joyous time for Fatima Jabbie-Bio. She engaged herself with celebrating her birthdays with the birthday cake as long as the palm tree in the presidential lodge with happiness. She did not even care about the calamities that our nation was encountering that we were going through in the country until when Almighty God intervened and calmed down the situation. Such a president's wife is a "green snake in the green grass awaiting to cause trouble that heads for death-meant for our SLPP." Only some of us who have detective eyes to see the nook note of her jubilation.

Fatima Jabbie-Bio cunningly undermined the women's wing of the vibrant SLPP-UK/I and for three years when it has been left dormant in silence. This unit has been replaced by

JMB-Women's movement raising a huge amount of money from SLPP followers, all went into Fatima Bio's personal account not audited or accounted for because she is highly respected as the president's wife. These DIRTY TRICKS between her legs and under her armpits now smell very disgusting to any of her very comforts and we are having any more of her NASTY TRICKS to allow her to hijack our SLPP and sell to the APC in the end, to get money.

The Hon Tamba Lamina got the awful smell of this JMB-Women first, as a sprinter group of SLPP women's wing unity. Now that SLPP has come to power, there should be no place for another women's wing. He gave this advice before taking up office as the Sierra Leone High Commissioner in UK in July 2019, but he was not listened to.

We must support the SLP to come back to power to rule for the third time continuously, to continue with the agenda of president Maada Bio. That is the only strategy that saves Sierra Leone from the APC.

All snakes are dangerous, and are instantly killed when found among human settlements. Snakes that cunningly sleep with human beings are after the destruction of their lives when the times come. Fatima Jabbie-Bio is just one of those snakes and our party SLPP is in very serious trouble because our son, father, brother, and president Julius Maada Bio has discovered himself sleeping with this snake cunningly since they met and she thinks that the time is now ripened when to silently kill and destroy our president and political party, the SLPP. Let us not accept it from her because we have known her DIRTY and TRICKS, very disgusting.

We will blame ourselves if we support her in her quests in search of political leadership in this method, for this country through marriage. She must fight and campaign for politics in her own county — The Gambia, where she was born. This evidence cannot be forged or changed as it is stated in her British naturalization passport, reserved for her easy accessibility back to UK in the case of trouble in Africa. Fatima Bio cannot be relied upon because she is like a parrot ready to fly and leave you behind to face your death because you don't have wings to fly out.

MY DEAR PEOPLE OF SIERRA LEONE, I HAVE NEVER BEEN INVOLVED IN NATIONAL POLITICS OF MY COUNTRY BUT IT IS NOW TIME FOR ME TO VOICE OUT MY WORDS TO EVERYBODY AND I WANT EVERYBODY TO LISTEN VERY CAREFULLY, TO THIS ONE-TO-ONE TALK TO YOUR HEART AS A TRUE SIERRA LEONEAN, ONE OF YOU.

I was sent to The Gambia by my then employers, the Institute of Commercial Management-(ICM), a British Educational Consultancy firm in 1989 at the height of the civil war in our country. This was in response to the then President Yahya Jammeh's to introduce that educational system in The Gambia. I spent five years there and returned in 2023 to join my family in the UK. I grew to like The Gambia, as a country, very much for the then head of state's gesture by accepting the Sierra Leonean refugees, running away from the civil war in their country. It was the civilized right thing to do for a neighbor in danger. Thank you president Yahya Jammeh for what your administration provided and may God always bless you.

Most of us were very happy and appreciative with the marriage of Maada Bio and Fatima but none of us think of their marrying to be ending up into selling our country to a Gambian national as Fatima now is pursuing. This kind of relationship is dangerous and detrimental to our country, which does not belong to president Julius Maada Bio as his personal property to be left in possession to his wife. We must make sure that this "sell-out" does not happen and dislike any political affiliation with Fatima Jabbie-Bio.

Kind regards to you all,

Mohamed Sannoh of Bongor Koya, Kenema District.

THE CIVIC EDUCATION METHODS RECOMMENDED FOR SIERRA LEONE, ESPECIALLY IN THE RURAL VILLAGES IN THE PROVINCES.

Has such an education project been implemented in Sierra Leone? The First Lady of Sierra Leone is more heard about in England and America than in our country. Why can she not spend some weeks working in the farms among people in the rural villages to actually learn from her experience what these people living in different communities go through rather than delivering her minds on political platforms which carry a different meaning to the people she is referring to? She will learn a lot from the village people, especially relating to the essence of earlier marriage.

Hence, this is classed as educational matters. Why can she not leave this project in the hands of the education ministry to professionally design her ideas and present them as an educational package to the right audience where it will become meaningful and beneficial to the country?

Therefore, the only solution to rectify the situation regarding primary and secondary school education is to establish an alternative examination system with the responsibility of assessing primary and secondary school education through an external examination system, in addition to the West African Examinations Council (WAEC) that was established in 1952. When these become open to competition and employment facilities, the frequency of examination leakages and future human intellectual damages will disappear.

WHAT SHOULD BE THE PENALTIES FOR GETTING SCHOOL GIRLS PREGNANT IN SIERRA LEONE?:

No girl on earth can become pregnant without having affairs with a man, except as it happened to the Virgin Mary when she got conceived of the baby Jesus. Even that it did not happened as a surprise to her. An Angel appeared to her to inform her about what was going to happen to her.(Luke 1:26-38). Therefore, the pregnant school girls in Sierra Leone are becoming pregnant not by surprise, but having matured male sexual partners, hence the Angel Gabriel is not appearing to them individually. Education is not a toy game to play with girls, until they become pregnant.Therefore, the pregnancies were the expected outcome and they were ready for the consequences without polluting the school environments where innocent children are gathered on daily basis to learn in their preparations of their future. *Now what were the government penalties on those men who interfered with these school girls and making them pregnant? What kind of provisions are "HANDS-OFF OUR GIRLS" making for these pregnant school girls?*

Are the pregnant school girls allowed to give birth in classrooms when they go to labour unexpectedly and in the process of the continuation of their education?

Let me explain explicitly to readers' understanding: A woman or a girl cannot make another woman or a girl pregnant even if they get involved in lesbian sexual relationship. ***A lesbian sexual relationship is when two or more than two women (females) without a man (Male) decide to have sex with each other at the same time to enjoy each other's sexual pleasure without involving a man or a male gender in the act.*** Science has not yet proved the possibility of getting any one of these sexual partners pregnant; except when a male-sperm is placed scientifically into the womb of a woman who does not want to have sex with a man. The pregnancies did not come to school girls in Sierra Leone as surprises because they were aware that by having sex, during when **a man penetrates his penis into the virginal of a woman to have sexual good times and pleasures,** such activities will eventually be resulted into getting the female pregnant and carry baby (babies) in her stomach until delivery.

Remember that this pregnancy is the first experience of these school girls and they could be unaware of the signs of danger that they are surrounded with. It is the duty of the Sierra Leone government to guide and protect them, and every school girl in Sierra Leone is part of the future of this country, but this is not the way to look after them.

They are innocent in this matter relating to their care as they are children themselves; school children. Is Maada Bio adding the provision of baby's crutches in every school when the pregnant school girls give birth to their babies to continue with their schooling?

Let me repeat myself here that if the acceptance of pregnant school girls in schools is a court ruling on the grounds of discrimination according to the report, I would like to recommend to the Sierra Leone government AN APPEAL against this court ruling or else, Maada Bio and his cabinet will be risking an embarrassment when this appeal is made through a higher court decision for a revocation of this court ruling through the International Court in The Hague by a Sierra Leone national who sees this as being unlawful and unfair to those school girls.

It appears that those working in the Ministry of Education, Science and Technology as well as the members of Maada Bio's cabinet are all "praise singers and hand clappers" as loudly as they can and perhaps under the influence of whisky and brandy. That is why there is no one bold enough to touch Maada Bio's shoulder and say "Please excuse me Sir," even when they see him mistakenly going in the wrong way.

Nobody cares as long as they know that their bread and butter is registered on the state expenses menu. Is this the way to run the affairs of a state?

As long as girls are able to identify men who get them pregnant, we'll expect that any male who interferes with underaged girls through sexual intercourse is dealt with severely through heavy fines of the law that I would recommend as follows, leading the men to hold responsibilities of:

---

1. *The girl's pregnancy treatment till her delivery by paying such bills to her parents/guardian's under whose care the girl survives.*
2. *The educational expenses for the girl directly to the girl's school, on her return to school until she completes her schooling and possibly her university education; (if she decides to continue to university or post-secondary education) rather than leaving the innocent girl damaged for life because of men sexual pleasure imposed on innocent girls. Although education system in Sierra Leone now operates on 'Quality Free Education' for all children, the Ministry of Education, Science and Technology will be in position to provide the amount of annual educational expenses government undertakes to sponsor each student and this will be used as landmark to determine how much will be the fine cost.*
3. *If the man cannot afford to provide this sponsorship for the girl he has impregnated through illegal and unauthorised sexual intercourse, the man should be arrested and imprisoned for a period of fifty (50) years but subject to parole after spending twenty five*

(25) years behind bars with hard labour. If in the process a member of his extended family happens to come forward and takes the responsibility for the payment of the fines, then the man should be released while the girl's educational sponsorship becomes the responsibility of the man who had sex with the girl that made her pregnant.

If the man who impregnates the girl is a 'school boy' with no employment or earning facilities, the same penalty of the law will also apply to him until his parents or member(s) of his extended family steps in to take up the financial responsibility accordingly

The girl's pregnancy treatment till her delivery by paying such bills to her parents/guardian's under whose care the girl survives.

The educational expenses for the girl directly to the girl's school, on her return to school until she completes her schooling and possibly her university education; (if she decides to continue to university or post-secondary education) rather than leaving the innocent girl damaged for life because of men sexual pleasure imposed on innocent girls. Although education system in Sierra Leone now operates on 'Quality Free Education' for all children, the Ministry of Education, Science and Technology will be in position to provide the amount of annual educational expenses government undertakes to sponsor each student and this will be used as landmark to determine how much will be the fine cost.

If the man cannot afford to provide this sponsorship for the girl he has impregnated through illegal and unauthorised sexual intercourse, the man should be arrested and imprisoned for a period of fifty (50) years but subject to parole after spending twenty five (25) years behind bars with hard labour. If in the process a member of his extended family happens to come forward and takes the responsibility for the payment of the fines, then the man should be released while the girl's educational sponsorship becomes the responsibility of the man who had sex with the girl that made her pregnant.

If the man who impregnates the girl is a 'school boy' with no employment or earning facilities, the same penalty of the law will also apply to him until his parents or member(s) of his extended family steps in to take up the financial responsibility accordingly.

Allowing pregnant school-girls to continue attending schools while under the stage of pregnancy will open Sierra Leone into Sex-Tourism getting our country into a mere sex-haven resort where sex pleasure hunters come to enjoy in kinky styles leaving all types of diseases. We have seen the rampant development of HIV/AIDS in some tourists resorts in some African countries and we do not want be like these countries.

We must understand that our country Sierra Leone have suffered from eleven years of civil war, leaving many girls without parents and the parents of these girls they are expected to turn to, for their upbringing is the government of the country.

Our country should not be campaigned and turned into a Tourist Resort for sexual pleasures of people who come from different parts of the world to have sex with our highly respected girls, our only Human Resources that we need to develop for our benefits.

My personal appeal to the SLPP government of President Julius Maada Bio is therefore to pay more attention to these orphan girls so that they will not feel like being LEFT BEHIND by our governments when they grow up in our society. They were born in Sierra Leone as human beings to be given humanly treatments and the Almighty God is making the provisions for these treatments through the governments of Sierra Leone. I don't think President Julius Maada Bio should disappoint these children.

We have heard too much shouting over the social media about 'Hands-Off Our Gils' but we are yet to see what are coming out of this laborious shouting. We are left to see if "the first lady" really means what she is shouting about, or is she using this to strategize her public attention to be taken notice of?

As government of today, leadership of the SLPP government will leave no stone unturned in the protection of these girls (most of whom are orphans) and indeed the future of the human capital resources of our country. It is our responsibilities jointly to ensure that they are shaped in a way that enables them to take all responsibilities of life caring, including state responsibilities at future strategic times.

President Maada Bio must understand that these school girls will not be able to become responsible citizens in Sierra Leone tomorrow if they are not prepared by providing them with the state cares and guidance's' in schools that they so desperately need today.

WARNING: Let me please bring to the attention of the government here that the arrival of the "Free Quality Education" in Sierra Leone is not a luxury but a necessity; and for ALL CHILDREN, including those from the families of opposition political party members. It is the responsibility of the Sierra Leone government to make the school environments attractive to the school children so that they will grow to love going to school every day and wear clean school uniforms. What makes school much more attractive to school children is making sure that they get their school meals (either free or at very low affordable costs) including clean water to drink.

When free food to eat in school is always available in our schools in Sierra Leone, it will be a motivating factor for the school children to love going to school on a daily basis and the doubts for wasting money on education will be eradicated. Until FREE EDUCATION is made compulsory and mandatory for all children in Sierra Leone, our government will be wasting money on education efforts and we will go nowhere.

This costs money, and if all children are not inc

Politicians themselves have gone through different classrooms under the instruction of different teachers and understand what I am talking here about. If the teaching profession is not encouraged and rewarded properly for the strains and difficulties that lie within, those who go to school will avoid this classroom profession and will be attracted to other different employments to live the easy lives.

Then my main question here is:
Long Lost "Stenophela"-Coffee Beans discovery in Sierra Leone

"HOW WILL FREE QUALITY EDUCATION TAKE PLACE WITHOUT GOOD QUALITY TEACHERS, AVAILABLE IN THE CLASSROOMS TO DELIVER FREE QUALITY EDUCATION in Sierra Leone?"

Long lost "Coffee-Beans" found in Sierra Leone.

The discovery of the long-lost Stenophylla coffee beans in the Ksmboi hills of the Eastern Province in Kenema District by researchers including Daniel Samu and colleagues from Kew Royal Botanic Gardens is received with joy in Sierra Leone but with great caution.

When Britain colonized Sierra Leone in 1787, their agricultural initiatives included planting coffee and cocoa beans, which they described as lasting cash crops providing a continuous source of income for Sierra Leonean farmers. The natives, lacking alternative employment and income sources, turned much of their fertile land into coffee and cocoa plantations, leaving little for rice farming, which remained community-owned under land tenure laws.

Coffee and cocoa beans have no food value locally except when exported for money determined by overseas markets.

My education in the UK has taught me about economic market practices: buyers and sellers meet to decide product values and negotiate prices they both accept. Coffee and cocoa beans are raw materials for high-value products in cold countries like the UK. I urge everyone to check prices of these commodities in local supermarkets such as Tesco and Sainsbury's to verify this.

I ask the Sierra Leone Parliament and House of Commons in London to recognize that Sierra Leoneans' eyes are now wide open regarding the trade practices involving their cash crops. Why are cash-crop farmers in Sierra Leone excluded from market negotiations over the prices of coffee and cocoa beans, which overseas buyers set unilaterally and impose on them? Can this be called fair trade?

Prices paid for coffee and cocoa beans have been systematically lowered compared to previous years, with buyers blaming international markets dominated by G7 countries—Canada, France, Germany, Italy, Japan, the UK, and the US, with the EU as guest participants.

Africa as a whole is absent from G7 discussions, including those concerning coffee and cocoa, although African countries supply raw materials that are key to these nations' consumable goods.

Where now lies the fairness of the fair trade in international trade including the G7 countries? They are right because the G7 countries behind the oceans of Africa are only interested in the African products to reach their shores and the markets, where they can treat African producers with all sorts of contents and dictations to their desires, whether the Africans like it or not. Was this the reasons why the colonial masters of Africa were so eager for their colonies in establishing the farms and plantations of these cash-crop farms in Africa? And now, farmers have no other alternative but to accept the

> ***This is a broad-day-light cheating of our African farmers, especially the cash crop producers in Sierra Leone because the producing of these agricultural products are manually done throughout the year, involving very high labour intensive inputs at all stages.***

Our politicians at the Tower Hill parliament are to be made aware of this and take it up, for example, with the House of Commons in London, the Capitol in the US, etc. otherwise, we have the right to re-use our fertile lands where coffee-beans and cocoa-beans are grown into planting different crops that can provide us, with direct consumable foods, such as rice, banana, plantain, cassava, breadfruits, yams and many others are awaiting to be discovered for our consuming advantages, that we can sell as well as provide foods our breakfast tables, especially during the raining seasons and can also prevent importation of food stuffs for individual consumptions in our country. We have to understand we are still "existence farmers" producing to exist (to enable us to survive) and not industrial purposes. Fighting and tearing-off pieces of papers in the chambers of the house over national census is not our priority in Sierra Leone.

The Horrors of African politics come from many angles surprisingly in different countries which are causing problems to education: The Chad case studies.

Chad is a large landlocked country spanning North-Central Africa, and one of the sahels including Bukina Faso, Cameroon, The Gambia, Mauritania, Mali, Niger, Nigeria and Senegal. Chad covers an area of 1,284,000 square kilometres (496,000 sq mi), lying between latitudes 7° and 24°N, and 13° and 24°E, and is the twentieth-largest country in the world. According to the 2019 population, the population of Chad is 15,000,000.

Chad has been extremely dangerous due to the risk of terrorism, kidnapping, unrest, and violent crime. The political leader who ruled Chad for 30 years since 1991 was Idriss Deby, with a military background, but he was recently killed by rebel fighters at a war front in a village on 19 April 2021. Violent conflict with armed rebels occurred in northern Chad following national elections on 11 April, approving Idriss Deby's rule for thirty-one consecutive years. Terrorist attacks are also a major risk in Chad, especially by the Nigerian militant group Boko Haram, according to the internet report of 22 April 2021.

The late president Idriss Deby's funeral took place at Chad's capital, N'Djamena, on 23 April 2021. He was 68 years old. His death has left many political observers in Africa questioning why President Idriss Deby went to fight the rebels at the war front rather than finding solutions to the rebel conflict in Chad, which has ravaged this part of the Sahel region for years.

Deby's son, Lt Gen Mahamat Idriss Déby Itno, has been named the new leader of Chad after his father's death during a battle with rebel forces.

Mahamat leads a 15-member Transitional Military Council (CMT) that will govern the country for the next 18 months.

He has a reputation for discretion and shunning the limelight, unlike some of his half-brothers. However, he is a battle-hardened soldier like his father. Mahamat, 37, is the same age as the late Déby was when he took power through a military coup in 1990.

Now, the young Mahamat's succession to his assassinated father has raised questions: What does Chad's political constitution say about political leadership succession? Has the leadership of the country become a family inheritance, granting automatic rights to Deby's son to continue, even temporarily, until final arrangements are made?

As rebel fighting continues, can Mahamat consider a peaceful resolution with rebel fighters through round-table discussions with all stakeholders in Chad, since these rebels are also Chadians with equal rights as citizens?

Will he continue to heed France's support by importing guns, bombs, and ammunition to kill Chadians—his own people? Will he continue viewing these Chadians as enemies of the state when they are from Chad? If he chooses this course, what impact will Chad's unrest have on Africa as a continent? What is the African Union doing about this? Is this not part of the African problems that make it difficult for Africans to live peacefully on the continent? Many Africans in the diaspora are hesitant to return home due to such instability. People have no individual voices unless echoing political powers, even when those powers err. This type of politics is a vicious horror circle in Africa!

I see the situation in Chad as an African problem because Chad is part of Africa. When one's toenail is painfully infected, the whole body is disturbed and unable to rest at night.

I recall my childhood in Sierra Leone, playing in dusty areas where lice thrived. These lice, parasites feeding on human flesh, when situated under toenails, make it impossible to sleep at night, as they become active then. These lice become what are locally called "Gigga." These Giggas dislocate toes to the point where wearing shoes becomes unbearable.

This condition can only be remedied when all Giggas are forcefully removed by one's mother, who cleans the feet thoroughly and applies ground pepper with salt to kill remaining germs and ties the feet in clean cloth until healed. Therefore, treating a boy's toes suffering from Gigga is not pleasant for either mother or child, but it is the only way to help the boy recover and stop him from playing in dusty places when unsupervised.

So, what has mother Africa got to do to her child Chad?

THE COMMON MISTAKES OF POLITICIANS IN AFRICA.

Almost all politicians in Africa make a common mistake starting from their inauguration day and state opening of parliaments when they come into power. Their mistake lies in the speeches filled with promises about what they will do during their tenure in all areas affecting human life. These speeches are often not written by themselves but by others. They simply read aloud from typewritten papers and receive the loudest applause of their lives. The danger is that these presidents do not fully understand the gravity of the promises they make, which they may not fulfill during their term.

Usually, after the speech, it is filed in record books or computer databases without being reviewed over time. Whether they deliver on their promises or stray off track, they do not care. Their concern is only to rally voters with political campaigns, loudspeaker talks from vehicles, to get re-elected so they can continue exploiting the people, draining them like sucking the marrow from Kentucky Fried Chicken bones during their five-year terms.

African politicians must realize that voters have heard enough inauguration speeches filled with promises and are now fed up.

Before voting for any politician's second term, we recall their earlier promises recorded as a tool to monitor their performance when first elected.

We are no longer willing to fight or make enemies; instead, we react through our votes in polling booths. We are human and need survival. What we need in Sierra Leone is FREE SCHOOL LUNCH for primary school children.

REDUCING FOREIGN ASSISTANCE: A BLESSING OR A CURSE?

African countries have relied on foreign aid since independence. Some U.S. programs, like the Millennium Challenge Corporation (MCC) and Africa Development Foundation (ADF), have successfully stimulated local economies and reduced aid dependency through sustainable agriculture, youth entrepreneurship, and better power access. Yet, foreign aid sometimes fosters dependency and paternalism instead of partnership. African governments should seize the opportunity to spur democracy and build prosperity via job creation, regional integration, and economic engagement.

PRIORITY NUMBER 1: JOB CREATION

Africa's youngest population is 200 million aged 15-24, doubling by 2045. A shortfall of 74 million jobs by 2020 demands policies nurturing competitive private sectors favoring business growth, job creation, sound fiscal and monetary policies, good governance, transparency, strong judiciary, better investment climates, and less corruption. Investments in private sector, infrastructure, manufacturing, and agriculture will address food insecurity and create jobs for youth. Improving education quality is key to building skilled workforces. Investors aiming to export agricultural produce from Sierra Leone while merely paying taxes are unwelcome. Food grown in Sierra Leone must benefit locals. Genetically modified seeds are prohibited to protect future agriculture.

PRIORITY NUMBER 2: REGIONAL INTEGRATION

Reducing Western aid requires enhancing regional integration to sustain development and prosperity. Intra-African trade boosts competition, productivity, and infrastructure. The African Continental Free Trade Area (CFTA), aiming for free trade among 54 states by 2017 and a continental union by 2019, marks a pivotal moment. Current intra-African trade is 12%, far below Europe's 60%, North America's 40%, and ASEAN's 30%. CFTA will create the world's largest single market and expand trade between African states by 50%.

Combined with good governance and stability, this will increase economic growth, jobs, poverty reduction, foreign direct investment, industrial development, and better global integration, reducing reliance on outside aid.

PRIORITY NUMBER 3: COMMERCIAL ENGAGEMENT AND TRADE

Africa's trade future depends more on its negotiation skills than its merits. U.S. trade reports highlight America's protectionist stance, but African Growth and Opportunity Act (AGOA) has created jobs in both the U.S. and Africa. The Trump administration may seek more reciprocal agreements, similar to EU-African Economic Partnership Agreements, favoring American exports.

Morocco's successful U.S. free trade agreement tripled American exports from $482 million in 2005 to $2.1 billion in 2015. Morocco's reforms positioned it as a gateway for U.S. companies to African and European markets, becoming the second-largest African investor after South Africa. Its return to the African Union and investment promises further growth.

African readiness for trade talks, such as with SACU and Egypt, remains limited. Greater dialogue within regional economic communities and with the U.S. is vital to accelerate reforms and increase trade.

As Ambassador Linda Thomas-Greenfield noted, Africa has made great democratic and economic progress and holds a growing global role. Policymakers must continue this trend by promoting African trade.

THE FUTURE OF U.S.-AFRICA ENGAGEMENT: TRADE, NOT AID?

Africa matters internationally for its resources, trade, economic opportunities, and long-term security. American engagement serves U.S. interests, as creating African jobs also affects global security. Youth unemployment fuels insurgency and trafficking, notably human smuggling into Europe.

Obama's Power Africa initiative created U.S. jobs by opening markets for U.S. energy companies, saving taxpayers money. The U.S. Trade and Development Agency increased energy project funding by 800%, boosting exports. Trump pursues policies offering maximum benefits to Americans. African leaders should not fear aid cuts but promote environments for local economy growth, attract investment, facilitate technology transfer, stimulate private sector competitiveness, and deepen regional integration.

Whether or not aid budgets shrink, Africa's prosperity depends on its own actions. U.S.-Africa relations should remain strong, bipartisan, and mutually beneficial. Mandela said, "It is always impossible until it is done."

Note: This blog reflects the views of the author only and does not reflect the views of the Africa Growth Initiative. Angelle B. Kwemo is managing director for Africa of Washington Media Group, Founder, Believe in Africa, and other author of "Against All Odds: How to Stay on Top of the Game."

THE "WHO-SAGA" ON CORONA VIRUS (COVID-19)

During a BBC-TV interview on 22 July 2021, the Director General of the World Health Organisation (WHO) Dr Tedros Adanom Ghebreyesus directly confirmed the sources of Covid-19 which has taken away so many lives in different parts of the planet, to the total of 4,155,011 as at 23 July 2021.

Dr Ghebreyesus confirmed that the sources of Covid-19 could have possibly originated from the Wuhan Institute of Technology in China, through leakages in this Chinese Scientific laboratory. He confirmed that "leakages from scientific laboratories are common and associated with laboratory practices, and also that he was a Lab-Technician himself, an Immunologist and had worked in a laboratory and lab accident. Is common. He has seen it happening and had upheld himself. So it can have happened".

This BBC interview statement from the WHO Director General himself has left different analysts, such as my very self, raising many questions about the purposes of Covid-19.

i. With all this kind of knowledge Dr Ghebreyesus had in the past about virology (which is the scientific discipline concerned with the study of the biology of viruses and viral diseases, including the distribution, biochemistry, physiology, molecular biology, ecology, evolution and clinical aspects of viruses), why did he not immediately introduce a total ban on China when the Corona Virus broke out in 2019, so that no one was allowed to enter the territory of China and no one was allowed to leave the territory of China, until the Covid-19 issue was professionally handled for the protection of the world?

ii. Why, in his capacity as the WHO Director General, did he embark upon campaigning on behalf of China to the rest of the world to “Show Solidarity” to China and cooperate with them on this catastrophic issue of the world? Was he using his position as the WHO Director General to politicize the coronavirus issue in the world while so many lives were at risk?

iii. As WHO is a wing of the United Nations formed in 1945 after the Second World War, as an international organisation of independent states, established to promote peace and international security, was this Covid-19 genuinely an accident that happened in China or a fulfilment of a Global Political Economy that had earlier been established by Prof. Robert O’Brien of Marc Master University in Canada and Prof. Marc Williams of the University of New South Wales in Australia in the third edition in 2010?

iv. Now that the world population is drastically reduced through deaths of humanity on the planet earth within a very short space of time, are world politicians now satisfied with how they can handle the world economy for human existence in observation of human rights issues, especially those relating to Africa?

Index. :

<u>SOME SECONDARY SCHOOLS IN THE NORTH, SOUTH and EASTERN PROVINCES OF SIERRA LEONE COVERED IN MY PREVIOUS EDUCATION RESEARCH</u>

1. A.D. Wurie Memorial Secondary School Lunsar Port Loko Sierra Leone West Africa.
2. Ahmadiyya Muslim Agricultural Secondary School Musa Road Kabala Sierra Leone West Africa Phone: +232 76 906018

3. Alhadi Islamic Vocational Secondary School Makeni Sierra Leone West Africa Phone: +232 76 688197 / +232 77 523511

4. Benevolent Islamic Secondary School Samaya Makeni Sierra Leone West Africa

5. Binkolo Catholic Secondary School Makeni Sierra Leone West Africa Phone: +232 76 705488

6. Bo Commercial School (Senior & Junior) Bo Sierra Leone West Africa
7. Holy Trinity Secondary School (Senior) Kenema, Sierra Leone - West Africa

8. Islamic Muslim Secondary School P O Box 177 Kenema Sierra Leone West Africa Phone: +232 76 646552

9. Kabala Secondary School (Senior) Kabala Sierra Leone West Africa

10. Kamaranka Secondary School Kamaranka Makeni Sierra Leone West Africa

11. Koidu Girls Secondary School Koidu Sierra Leone West Africa

12. Mandu Secondary School Mobai Kailahun Sierra Leone West Africa

13. Martilie International School Off Regent Road Hill Station Freetown Sierra Leone West Africa

14. Methodist Secondary School Kenema Sierra Leone
    a. West Africa Phone: +232 76 658524

15. Milton Computer Secondary School Bo Sierra Leone West Africa

16. Murialdo Secondary School Makeni Sierra Leone West Africa

17. Narrat Jahr Ahmadiyya School Bo Sierra Leone West Africa

18. National Secondary School Kailahun Sierra Leone West Africa

19. Pendembu Vocational Technical Secondary School Kailahun Sierra Leone West Africa

20. Queen of the Rosary School Bo Sierra Leone West Africa

21. Scarcies Baptist Secondary School/strong Makeni Sierra Leone West Africa

22. S.l.M.B. Secondary School/strong Pendembu Kailahun Sierra Leone West Africa

23. St. Francis Secondary School (Junior) Makeni Sierra Leone - West Africa, Phone: +232 76 722818

24. Tahir Ahmadiyya Muslim Secondary School Bo Sierra Leone West Africa
25. Wuroh Memorial Secondary School Makeni Sierra Leone West Africa

26. Ahmadiyya Secondary School Kabala Sierra Leone West Africa

27. Ahma M. Secondary School Koribondo Bo Sierra Leone West Africa

28. Birch Memorial Secondary School, Makeni Sierra Leone West Africa Phone: +232 76 621472
    a. B.I.S.S. School (Senior) Makeni Sierra Leone West Africa

29. Bo Government Secondary School Bo Sierra Leone West Africa Phone: +232 76 646470

30. Foundation for School Leavers Advocacy and Development Org 27 Blama Road Kenema - Sierra Leone, West Africa Phone: +232 76 950942

31. Government Secondary School (Senior) Koyeima Bo Sierra Leone West Africa

32. Holy Trinity Secondary School (Junior) Kenema Sierra Leone West Africa

33. Harrkem Islamic Secondary School Makeni Sierra Leone - West Africa

34. Jawie Ahmadiyya Secondary School Daru Kailahun Sierra Leone West Africa

35. Kakuwa Youth Training Centre 32 Musa Street Bo Sierra Leone West Africa

36. Loma Secondary School Kabala Sierra Leone West Africa

37. Marampa Islamic Secondary School Lunsar Port Loko Sierra Leone West Africa

38. M.C.A. School (Senior) Makeni Sierra Leone West Africa

39. Methodist High School Bo Sierra Leone West Africa Phone: +232 76 644132

40. 20. M.S.S.B. School Magburaka Sierra Leone West Africa Phone: +232 76 608402

41. Nasir Ahmadiyya Secondary School Kenema Sierra Leone Phone: +232 33 840983
42. Pampana High School Makeni Sierra Leone West Africa

43. St. Francis Secondary School (Senior) Makeni Sierra Leone West Africa
44. St. Joseph's Secondary & Agricultural School P O Box 70 Blama Road - Blama Sierra Leone

West Africa

<u>Bibliography:</u>

(1976) A. Hailey, Doubleday – Penguin BooksUK

(2013) A. K. Kamara, The Collapse of Educational Standards in Sierra Leone (Commentary) Patrioticvanguard, Toronto, Canada.

J.Evers and R Kneyber (2016 Flip The System.

(2003) Paraka Jr. J.D, New York, Routledge *The Athens of West Africa: A History of International Education at Fourah Bay College, Freetown, Sierra Leone.*

(2010) D. Ravitch, The death and life of the great American School System: Basic Books, PA 19103 USA

(2013) Pearl, N.V. The Power of Positive thinking: Fireside Books, USA

(2017) J. J. Bangura, The Temne of Sierra Leone: African Agency in the making of a British Colony, New York: Cambridge University Press

(1969) E. S. Sawyer The Development of Education in Sierra Leone In Relation To Western Contact.

Holy Bible: Luke 1:26-38

(2020) Woodward, B RAGE *Simon & Schuster, UK.*

www.cambridge.org/core/journals/history-in-africa

www.22011-2014, Education for change programmes in Sierra Leone in 2019 published in the IBIS document

"Education for Development" the Education for Sector (EFC) .

www.intechopen.com/online-first/mathematics-education-system-in-south-africa

https://en.wikipedia.org/wiki/Ellen_Johnson_Sirleaf

www.google.com/search?safe=strict&source=hp&ei=1uLzXJelBM .

www. https://revisesociology.com/2017/10/24/the-1988-education-reform-act-class-notes/

www.theguardian.com/commentisfree/2012/mar/23/tunisia-women-revolution

Necessary Datelines to remember as extracted from the internet.

1884, Mechanics Alliance trade union is formed.

1885, Carpenters Defensive Union (trade union) formed.

1893, army barracks workers strike in Freetown; other workers stage sympathy strike. Governor Fleming swears-in 200 special constables to suppress it.

1919. Strike and riot. Railway and Public Works department strikes, in part "on account of the nonpayment of War Bonus gratuities to African workers, although these had been paid to other government employees, especially European personnel." Major riots occur in Freetown. The Creole intelligentsia remain neutral.

1920, Sierra Leone Railway Skilled Workmen Mutual Aid Union formed.

1923–1924. Moyamba riot.

1925. The 1920 union is renamed the Railway Workers' Union.

1926. Strike and riot. Railway Workers' Union strikes January 13 to February 26. Rioting erupts in Freetown. Creole intelligentsia supports the strikers. According to Wyse this is the first time workers and intelligentsia acted in harmony. The strike was viewed as a threat to stability by the government, and suppressed by troops and police

1930. Kambia riot.

1930–1931.Haidara Kontorfilli rebellion, named after its charismatic Muslim leader. Wyse gives the causes as "heavy handedness of chiefly rule and the deteriorating social and economic conditions, as well as the erosive nature of colonial rule." Ended after Kontorfilli was killed by British forces

1931. Pujehun riot

1934. Kenema riot.

1938–39. Series of strikes and civil disobedience. WAYL blamed.

1939. Army mutiny. January, led by Creole gunner Emmanuel Cole.

1948. Riot at Baoma Chiefdom of Bo District. One hundred people committed for trial before supreme court for their part in it

1950, October. African United Mine Workers' Union (Secretary-General was Siaka Stevens) strikes in Marampa and Pepel, Northern Province. Strikers riot and burn the house of the African personnel officer.

1950, 30 October, Kailahun. 5,000 people riot. Cause was a rumour that the Paramount Chief of Luawa Chiefdom would be upheld and reinstated by the government.

1951. Pujehun, South Eastern Province.

3 March: Armed attack at night on chief's house repelled by police.

15 March: Several villages refuse to pay house tax to government unless chief deposed. Intimidation practised on government sympathisers.

2 June: About 300 "rioters" from outlying villages attack the town of Bandejuma. 101 people committed for Supreme Court trial. Others dealt with summarily.

1955, February. Freetown General Strike over rising cost-of-living and low pay. Lasted several days: looting, property damage, including residences of government ministers. Leader: Marcus Grant.

1955–56 riots. From the Northern province district of Kambia to the South-Eastern Pujehun district. "It involved 'many tens of thousands' of peasants and hinterland town dwellers."

FINALLY, and FINALLY

The facts about our country, Sierra Leone's backwardness in education including all structures relating to developments to move us forward has seriously undermined by the formation of the All Peoples Congress (APC) political party which Siaka Stevens founded on 20 March 1960.

APC removed the railway transportation in this country that the British, our colonial masters left with us; instead of developing or making all facilities to make it going. He replaced the railways with the road systems and gave huge contracts to the Chinese company, "WaanmanAbu" who did not do good jobs as expected and he did not care, because the railway was great benefit to farmers in the Kailahun, Kenema and Bo districts for heavy transfer of cocao and coffee harvests to Freetown port for shipping.

The same APC also systematically undermined the school education facilities in our country to the level of letting school children in our country carry their own desks and chairs to be used in their class learning. I was teaching at the Methodist Boys' High School in 1987 when the APC was under the administration of J.S.Momoh; so I am explaining as an eye-witness reporter. The essence of this rip-off was meant to make education difficult for the poor young Sierra Leoneans. The Magboraka Boys' Secondary School of the St. Francis fame was seriously damaged and reduced to a bin under APC's Ernest Koroma. Education facilities were opened to children whose parents were connected to APC political party and most of us never enter FBC in our Sierra Leone. I will like to draw everybody's attention to the present dilapidated condition of the "Women Teachers College in Port Loko which came out disgracefully on social media coverage.

Now that the SLPP under President Julious Maada Bio, we the SLPP members have discovered the right time to reverse the clock back to the right direction. Let us unite to keep the SLPP in power to keep the progressive and development agenda which the president has initiated, particularly for the young Sierra Leoneans to get good FREE QUALITY EDUCATION. The APC never thought of this kind of initiative for the future of Sierra Leone to avoid money grabbing opportunities.

KKY & FATIMA JABIE-BIO, ARE MAKING LOVE BEHIND OUR PRESIDENT BIO'S BACK. LET THE PUBLIC KNOW ABOUT THIS UNLAWFUL ROMANCES IN OUR COUNTRY, SIERRA LEONE: THERE IS NO SECRET ABOUT THEIR DIRTY RELATIONSHIPS:

Fatima Jabie-Bio, the wife of our president is not committed to SLPP anymore, but to APC as per her linkages with Olayinka Sylvia Blyden and Yvonne Aki Sawyer. She is putting heavy weights now to KKY-Kandeh Kolleh Yumkella (KKY) to become flag bearer for SLPP to choose her into his running mate.

We don't hate KKY, but it is just difficult to accept him to take over leadership of the SLPP because of his past, by leaving our party to form his own political party, taking huge number of voters and supporters away for SLPP. KKY's plan was to get SLPP into trouble, to loss.

It is now time for him to realise that the SLPP members are not as stupid as he thought. We are quite educated enough to read between the lines of "SaLone" politics even if some of us who votes legally and constructively don't have PhD letters after our names.

KKY has proved to us that he is not reliable and dependable. We are not stupid to leave our party in the dirty hands of a leader who does not care for us because of his UN work experience. If he wants to be a party leader, let him lead his very own National Grand Coalition(NGC) political party he has already formed.

KKY & Fatima Bio's strategy is they both jointly want to create a very heavy force to win the Flag-Bearer for KKY who is not in the interest of SLPP. After box-upping, mixing and destabilizing SLPP, they jointly sell our political party votes to APC and leave us, the poor Sierra Leone Peoples Party (SLPP) supporters in the sufferings we are managing to avoid under Maada Bio's administration. Maada Bio is not working alone. He is working with the inspiration of the HOLY SPIRITS from Heaven but tormented by these evil spirits who are agents of the devil in hell.

LET US DON'T MAKE THIS POSSIBLE!

Finally, let the SLPP supporters be aware that if the Flag-Bearer of our party becomes a problem of internal issue in our party, the president also has the right to make changes to our national constitution in our country, Sierra Leone. This change will give mandate to the present president to be elected again for the third time, in the expected and awaiting general election in 2028. There will be no horror for President Julious Maada Bio to remain as president for Sierra Leone for the third time as long as the majority of the voters say so in the democratic election box; and due to the good education changes he has initiated and implemented.

The only other problem the whole country, particularly the SLPP members and supporters will expect is with the First Lady Fatima, who may insist on her crying in her dreams because she wants to inherit our presidency again, through marriage to a foreigner who has claimed to be a Gambian as her country of birth and not a Sierra Leonean according to her dual nationality status with the UK. If President Bio can promise to put his wife under control as a Sierra Leonean woman can behave, they will both live in perfect peace in his third term of office.

MAY THE ALMIGHTY GOD REMAIN TO BLESS THE SIERRA LEONE PEOPLES' PARTY-SLPP, IN SIERRA LEONE ALWAYS

www.ingramcontent.com/pod-product-compliance
Lightning Source LLC
LaVergne TN
LVHW010611100826
845148LV00014B/2916
9781535605083